My ZOMBIE Hamster

My ZOMBIE Hamster

Havelock McCreely

EGMONT USA
New York

EGMONT

We bring stories to life

First published by Egmont USA, 2014
443 Park Avenue South, Suite 806
New York, NY 10016

1 3 5 7 9 8 6 4 2

www.egmontusa.com

Library of Congress Cataloging-in-Publication Data
McCreely, Havelock, 1975-
My zombie hamster / Havelock McCreely.
pages cm -- (My zombie hamster)
Summary: Matt Hunter is expecting the latest sword-and-fantasy video
game, but he's in for a disappointment when he receives a hamster for
Christmas instead. A hamster called Snuffles. A hamster that dies, but
somehow keeps going. A zombie hamster that has his eye on Matt.
ISBN 978-1-60684-491-5 (hardback) -- ISBN 978-1-60684-492-2 (eBook)
[1. Hamsters--Fiction. 2. Zombies--Fiction. 3. Family life--Fiction.
4. Friendship--Fiction. 5. Humorous stories.] I. Title.
PZ7.M47841455My 2014
[Fic]--dc23   2014008384

Printed in the United States of America

To Caroline, Bella, and Caeleb.

You know who you are
and you know why.

Havelock

TUESDAY, DECEMBER 24
Christmas Eve

Christmas Eve is when they change the voice tracks on the Zombie Zappers. Or Zee-Zees, as everyone calls them.

They're not really called that. The proper name for a Zee-Zee is Undead Neutralization Unit, or U.N.U. for short. Which is typical of the lack of imagination in adults. They don't think these things through. These things need to roll off the tongue. They need to be catchy. I mean, how much cooler would it be if they'd called them Zombie Atomizer Pods?

Z.A.P.s!

Or Deceased Eradication and Annihilation Devices?

D.E.A.D.s!

I think you'll agree: *much* better.

The Zombie Zappers are pretty much exactly what they sound like. You know those little bug killers people hang on their porches during summer? The bugs see this beautiful UV light, fly straight at it, then *bzzt!*—instant fried bug?

The Zee-Zees work the same way. Except, instead of bugs, they attract zombies, and, instead of UV light, they use recordings of human voices. The zombies are attracted to these juicy sounds of life, wander into one of the Zee-Zees expecting lunch, and bye-bye zombie.

I should probably explain about the zombies. (Or deadbeats, as everyone calls them.) There's a chance this journal will be picked up centuries in the future and you might not know about them.

What can I say? They've been around since before I was born. I've never known anything else. Not like my parents. They talk about "before," when they could walk around in the countryside, or travel from one side of the U.S. to the other without fear of being overrun by crazed, flesh-eating monsters. (Although, when I asked them if they'd ever done any of those things, they got annoyed and said that wasn't the point. The point was that they *could* have. Even though they hadn't.)

It's a tradition that the voices of the Zee-Zees are provided by the inhabitants of the town they protect. The winners are picked by lottery, and every Christmas Eve we're treated to a performance of the new voices that will run all the next year.

This Christmas Eve was a big one for my family, because my dad had won a place on the voice track. (At least, that's what *he* thought.) He'd spent the better part of six months coming up with what he planned to say, keeping it a secret from all of us. Even Mom. (No mean feat, let me tell you.)

The whole town had gathered for the unveiling of the voice tracks. The families of those who won the lottery were allowed to watch from the top of the twenty-foot-high, ten-foot-thick wall that surrounded Edenvale. While I stood there waiting for the event to get going, shivering and slapping my arms in an attempt to keep warm, I caught a glimpse of Charlie down below.

Charlie's my best friend, along with Calvin and

Aren, but I couldn't see them anywhere. We've known each other since kindergarten, when someone tried to steal my plastic shovel and she shoved his head into the sand until he begged for mercy.

I waved down at her. A second later my phone erupted with the sound of a lightsaber igniting. I opened the message to find an animated image of a rotting deadbeat with its eyes dangling out of its sockets. The caption underneath the zombie read: "What you looking at, ugly?"

I glanced down and saw Charlie grinning up at me. She was never happier than when she was insulting someone.

My mom flicked the back of my head. "Put that away. It's about to start."

I turned around to join the others. Outside the walls, on the mile-wide stretch of snow-covered grass that circled our town, were the Zombie Zappers. They looked like . . . well, they looked like portable toilets, to be honest. Green, upright structures barely big enough for one person to stand inside.

Our mayor cleared his throat. One of his aides quickly assembled a small portable stage for him and helped him climb up. (The mayor was really short. Really, really short.) He now towered above us all, framed against the gray sky.

As always, the mayor was clutching his dog in his arms. (The dog's name is Pugsley, and it's a pug. Yes, Pugsley the pug. As you can see, our mayor is not known for his imagination.) The mayor started his speech, which went on for a long time. A really long time. ". . . count ourselves lucky, remember the fallen, yada yada yada."

My eyelids drooped and my mouth fell open. My brain actually went into screen-saver mode. I only snapped out of it when the drool started to freeze on my lip.

Finally, it was time for the unveiling of the new voices.

The first recording to echo from the speakers of the Zee-Zees was a boring poem about life before the deadbeats arrived.

The next track was a long, really bad song about a time in the not-too-distant future when deadbeats and humans would all just get along and we could return to nature like the happy, peaceful people we all were.

It was terrible, but the zombies seemed to like

it. While the song played, a few of them shuffled out of the distant forest, shambling slowly toward the town wall. (Looking like my dad when he gets up in the morning.)

I say "like it," but perhaps they just hated folk music and wanted to eat the singer.

The third voice was simply a list of names of those who had fallen in the zombie war. This was greeted with bowed heads and silence.

Then it was Dad's turn. He straightened proudly and grinned at me.

"You'll like this, Matt," he said.

I'm just going to pause here for a second. *Yes*, what I did was wrong, and possibly mean. But it was funny, and funny makes up for a lot.

You see, I spied on my dad. I knew what he had planned for his voice track. He was going to read a short story he had written. Some kind of reversal on what really happened, where the deadbeats were now in charge and the humans were locked out in the forests.

This kind of thing didn't go down well with the mayor's office. Or the Zombie Police. I mean, I'd already seen them giving dirty looks to the folk-singer.

So, really, I'd been protecting my family from major embarrassment.

Plus, I'd listened to Dad read his story out loud. It was a good story, I'll give him that. (My dad's a writer, after all.) But it lasted for *forty-five minutes*, and if he thought I was standing up here in the freezing cold for that long, he was farther gone than I'd thought.

So I switched recordings. I'd made my own voice track after watching some of Dad's old action movies and replaced the files my dad was sending to city hall.

I did it for him.

Well, that's not really true. I did it for me. But it *benefited* him.

There was a moment of silence before the unveiling, then my voice echoed loud and clear over the speakers.

"Bring it on, zombie scum!"

"Right this way for the magical carpet ride . . . of death!"

"Fresh meat! Fresh meat!"

"Roll up! Win a prize every time . . . the prize of death!"

Hmm. Not great, that one. I was losing a bit of

inspiration by this time. But still—not bad.

At this point, I was doubled over with laughter. But then I noticed the silence spreading out around me. That very particular silence you get when you've done something wrong and it's been discovered.

I stopped laughing and straightened up. Mom was glaring at me with that special look of hers, and everyone else was shaking their heads and making *tut-tut* noises. Charlie was laughing hysterically. Dad was trying to look angry, but I could see he was holding in a grin.

See, that's the thing about my dad. He's not truly a grown-up. I don't think he passed the test they give out when you're supposed to become a real adult.

Everyone was so busy glaring at me that no one actually noticed the deadbeats. They'd reacted to my voice track and were heading straight toward the Zee-Zees. Not only that, but it seemed my voice was drawing more out of the trees also. Maybe the zombies liked the same movies my dad did.

The first deadbeat arrived at the Zee-Zee directly below us and stumbled inside with a drawn-out moan. There was a bright flash of light, an electrical hum, then a sad little wisp of smoke drifted up into the gray sky.

I lifted my hands in the air and did a little victory dance.

Then Mom grabbed my ear and dragged me back home.

WEDNESDAY, DECEMBER 25
The Christmas of D-o-o-o-o-o-m

10:00 a.m. So far, today has been a total waste of time. I don't know why I even bother asking for presents. Every year it's the same thing.

"Matt," my mom says, "what do you want Santa to bring you?"

And every year since I was eight, I give my mom a look of utter scorn that she fails to recognize and tell her what I want Santa to bring.

Then on Christmas morning I unwrap a gift that is light-years away from what I asked for.

I'm not talking slightly different here, like the kind of mistake you expect parents to make. (For instance, asking for Runespell 5 and being given the expansion pack for Runespell 4 instead.) That kind of thing is expected. You clear a spot on your day-after-Christmas schedule to head off to the mall on an exchange run, where you join the lines of others doing exactly the same thing.

No, what I'm talking about is so extreme it can only be intentional. I reckon my parents are either, A: experimenting on me, to see what kind of adult they can create by constantly disappointing me as a child, or B: they've laid bets on how long it will take for me to break down and ask to see a shrink.

This year I asked for the Runesword that would let me play Runespell without the control pad. (My cleric is twenty-eighth level, and I've been playing him for two years now.) Charlie, Calvin, and Aren are all asking for the same thing, and we planned on spending Christmas afternoon playing online.

Guess what I got. Go on. I bet you'll never get it.

Give up?

Fine.

I got a hamster.

I'm not even kidding.

A hamster.

Called Snuffles.

I stared at my parents as they stood next to

the Christmas tree. I thought it was some kind of joke, that they would step aside with a flourish and shout "Surprise!" as they handed over the sword.

No such luck. Instead, they stared at me expectantly with big smiles on their faces.

"We know it's not what you asked for," said Mom.

A million points to Mom for stating the obvious.

Dad stepped in. "But your mother—that is, *we*—thought this would be better for you," he said. "Teach you how to look after something, to nurture another living being. That kind of thing."

I didn't want to nurture another living being! I wanted to cut down hordes of goblins with a plastic sword! Why couldn't people understand that? It was a very simple concept.

I looked at Snuffles. He was standing on his hind legs, staring at me with eyes as black as a shark's. I got the distinct feeling he was laughing at me.

Still, I didn't want to hurt their feelings, so I forced a smile onto my face. "Um . . . thanks?"

But because I had to express my disappointment somehow, I decided to resort to a bit of passive-aggressiveness.

"I'll just watch him on his wheel while Charlie and the others are fighting goblins and orcs with their swords."

I should have known that kind of thing was too subtle for them.

"You see?" Mom said to Dad. "I told you he'd prefer a hamster to a stupid sword."

Dad said nothing, but I noticed the brief look of shame that flashed across his face.

He knew! He knew how I would feel about the hamster, and he caved in to Mom.

I'd make him pay for that.

I looked at Katie's presents. No Christmas morning disappointment for her. She got the huge dollhouse she asked for as well as the really expensive dolls that went with it.

Was that fair?

1:00 p.m. My mom's sister, Aunt Carla, and Gran arrived while Mom was preparing Christmas dinner.

Gran's first words when she came through the door were, "Smells like something's burning."

Mom sprinted to the kitchen to check on the turkey. Gran smiled at me while Aunt Carla looked around her with her usual expression of disapproval. (She looks like she's constantly sucking on a lemon. Her mouth is all pursed and frowny.) She ran her finger over the bannister, checking for dust. Muffled wails erupted from the kitchen.

It had started.

2:00 p.m. My mom must have inherited her gift-giving genes from Gran. Katie got gift vouchers to spend on whatever she wanted. I was really happy when I saw that. I could put them toward buying the Runesword I wanted.

But my destiny in life is to be constantly disappointed. Mom and Gran must have conspired, because Gran got me one of those weird hamster houses. You know, the ones that have the two holes in the casing that you attach all those plastic tubes to. You're supposed to spend your allowance on buying more of the tubes and make all those weird shapes so the hamster can climb through them and have "hours of hamstery fun," as the box puts it.

"Can I trade it in for the cash instead?" I asked.

Mom opened her mouth, probably to shout at

me, but before she could say anything there was a heavy knock at the door.

☀

2:30 p.m. A few minutes later, we (and everyone else in the street) had been herded out of our houses and told to stand in the freezing cold, hopping from foot to foot while tall, scary officials dressed head to toe in black body armor ordered us around like cattle.

Our street was undergoing a surprise Zombie Squad inspection.

The Zombie Squad's job is to make sure that everyone who said they were alive really was alive and hadn't passed away and turned into a zombie or something.

That was everyone's greatest fear: a deadbeat turning up *inside* Edenvale's walls.

"The longer you complain, the longer this will take!" shouted the leader of the squad. He wore a black helmet with a tinted visor covering the top half of his face. He looked a bit like RoboCop. Or Judge Dredd.

"It's Christmas Day!" said Mom, who happened to be first in line. "Why didn't you do this last week?"

The man tilted his head down and stared at Mom. He probably expected this to intimidate her, but he obviously didn't know my mom.

"I'm cooking Christmas dinner," she said. "You didn't even let me turn the oven off. If my turkey burns I'm suing you."

"Ma'am, do you think I *want* to be here? Don't you think I'd rather be at home with my own family on Christmas Day?"

Mom softened slightly, and the Zombie Squad leader bared his teeth in what might have been a smile.

"But I don't have a family, do I? So to answer your question, yes, we could have done this last week, but it's easier for us to do it today. Everyone gathered at their homes on Christmas Day? Makes our job a hundred times easier. Wrist!"

Mom bit her tongue and held out her wrist. The Zombie Squad leader ran a handheld device over the lifechip embedded deep beneath her skin, then read the display.

"Emma Hunter. Husband. Three children. Where is your family?"

We raised our hands, and he ran the device

very slowly over our lifechips.

"Says here you're all still alive. Well done."

"Of course we're alive, you idiot!" snapped Gran. "You can see that!"

He turned to Gran. "Can't always trust the eyes, ma'am. You could be a new breed of particularly cunning zombie. Have to make sure."

The Zombie Squad officer ran the scanner over Gran's wrist and read the display. Then he did it again, just to be on the safe side.

I should point out that Zombie Squad officers aren't really known for their sharp wits. They're more like a volunteer police force. Normal people with a craving for power. I imagine the entry exams go something like this.

Entry Exam for Being a Zombie Squad Person

QUESTION 1: Are you a zombie? (Cross out wrong answers.)

ANSWER: ~~Yes~~. ~~No~~. Unsure.

QUESTION 2: Do you like bossing people around?

ANSWER: Yes. ~~No~~. ~~Unsure~~.

Congratulations. You're hired.

3:00 p.m. Christmas dinner. Dry turkey. Lumpy gravy. Overcooked vegetables. Gran gleefully prodding her food and declaring it inedible.

Mom not happy.

SNUFFLES WATCH: Snuffles slept all day, waking up only to stuff his cheeks full of food before returning to his bed.

Maybe we have some things in common after all.

THURSDAY, DECEMBER 26

Spent the day in bed playing video games. (With the control pad! Can you believe it?) But I didn't have any peace. Mom kept telling me to get up and do something productive.

"Like you?" I asked.

"Yes. Like me."

So I asked her if she wanted me to watch celebrity gossip on TV, read about it in a magazine, or talk about it on the phone for an hour to her friend.

She left me alone after that.

It's reached a certain point in my dad's work cycle. I've mentioned before that Dad is a writer. He writes these pulp science fiction books featuring a guy called Atticus Pope. He's on the fifth book right now, which has something to do with Atticus fighting Nazis on the moon. (You can tell my dad really loves the Indiana Jones and James Bond movies. His books are the same kind of thing. Atticus Pope foiling evil guys bent on stealing something priceless or taking over the world.)

But when Dad gets really into writing his books, he goes into a world of his own, wandering around the house in his robe, a toy gun in his hand, acting out the scenes before he writes them down. It's very funny to watch.

He wandered out into the front yard once when he was really stuck on a book, testing out scenes, then shaking his head and trying out different versions. Mom filmed him on her phone and played it back to show him how ridiculous he looked. But if she thought it was going to embarrass him into stopping, she was very much mistaken. He watched the video silently, jumped up, gave Mom a kiss on the cheek, and said she'd solved the problem for him. Atticus needed a love interest who betrays him.

Then he disappeared into his office for the

rest of the afternoon. Mom wasn't particularly impressed.

I've read Dad's books. They're pretty good. A bit old-fashioned, though. All ray guns and rocket ships. But he did give me permission to write a screenplay based on the stories.

I tried, but to be honest, it was pretty hard work, so I scrapped that idea and have been writing an original screenplay based on Atticus Pope. I'll show it to Dad once it's finished. I'm sure he'll think it's amazing. In fact, I reckon he'll want to adapt my screenplay into his next Atticus Pope book.

I wonder how much he'll pay me for that?

SNUFFLES WATCH: Snuffles escaped from his cage. Don't ask me how. Have searched everywhere but can't find him. Haven't told anyone yet. Contemplated buying a replacement before Mom and Dad notice. Realized I can't. All the paperwork. Registering the pet, getting an all clear on the lifechip, that kind of thing. Plus, you need a guardian's signature to own any kind of animal.

FRIDAY, DECEMBER 27

I'm getting worried about Katie. She's always been a bit odd, but recently she's been getting a lot worse.

Mom told me to call her for lunch. I did what I usually do, which is to scream out her name at the top of my lungs. Mom threw a dish towel at my face and told me to go and get her.

What is it with parents and unnecessary exercise? Or rather, what is it about parents forcing unnecessary exercise on their children? If we'd *both* shouted, Katie would have heard us, but instead of us putting our heads together to come up with a solution to the problem, Mom orders me to do uncalled-for physical exercise. I get enough of that at school!

I found Katie staring at herself in the mirror, with tears streaming down her face.

I asked her what was wrong. Our eyes locked in the mirror. There was a brief pause, and then she said in a low, sepulchral (I looked that word up in the dictionary; it fits perfectly) voice, "Nothing's wrong. I just like the taste of tears."

I grinned and nodded as if I hadn't heard a thing. "Well, that's good. Lunch is ready," I said, then bolted back downstairs.

Weird.

SNUFFLES WATCH: Snuffles is back in his cage, sleeping under a pile of sawdust. He must have gotten bored and returned home. That's a relief. Won't have to explain to Mom and Dad how I managed to lose him after only a couple of days.

SATURDAY, DECEMBER 28

Besides Charlie, I have two other best friends, Calvin and Aren. (We all live on the same street, so I suppose it was natural that we formed a group.) I mentioned them before, but I thought I should describe them a bit more here.

Calvin is . . . how should I put it? He's a bit slow.

For instance, when he types searches into the Web, even Google doesn't know what he's actually trying to spell.

His brother once convinced him you could buy nonstick glue so there wasn't any gooey mess on your fingers, and he spent an entire day going from store to store asking if they stocked it.

Oh, and my personal favorite. He thought his

orange juice was trying to send him psychic messages because the carton said "concentrate" on the side. He'd stare at it for half an hour straight, just waiting for a sign. I asked what he thought was going to happen, and he said he was unsure. Either an alien race was going to contact him or his future self had discovered a method of communicating with him in the past and was going to send him messages that would make him rich.

Aren is the complete opposite. His parents are originally from Nigeria. They moved here before the zombie outbreak. Aren is so clever it's scary. He watches *MythBusters* and tells us where the guys on the show went wrong with their testing. Which, to me, is amazing, because all of my science knowledge is taken from *MythBusters*. After each episode I text him to ask if he thinks they did it right.

Both guys came around today, and guess what? They both got the Runeswords! No Christmas character-building for them.

Life is so unfair.

SUNDAY, DECEMBER 29

I hate Sundays. I always have.

Well, not always. But ever since I started school I've hated Sundays. There is a program here that has been on forever. One of those current-affairs-filled-with-bad-news programs. Every Sunday evening at seven o'clock, its horrible, fateful music starts playing, and that's when you know your weekend is officially over. That homework can't be put off for another second.

And you can't even ignore it at the beginning of the weekend. The makers of the show start pushing out their promos on Friday night. So even before you've had a chance to collapse on the couch and contemplate the glorious weekend stretching ahead of you, a commercial appears with that horrible, depressing music to warn you that Sunday is only a matter of hours away.

It's like those stores that have back-to-school promotions three weeks into summer vacation. It shouldn't be allowed.

When I become Grand High Overseer of the World I'll make sure that kind of thing is banned for good. (I contemplated becoming President, but then thought, why limit myself? Grand High Overseer of the World sounds so much better.)

I've started putting a list together of all the things I'll change.

List of Annoying Things I Will Change When I Am Declared Grand High Overseer of the World

1. No running ads for Sunday-night shows on Friday. No exceptions.
2. No advertising back-to-school specials three weeks into summer vacation. (I'm going to have to invent a special punishment for those stores that

use the slogan "Back2School" in any advertisement. It's one of those things that really annoys me.)

3. Every house is to be fitted with intercoms in each room. (That way I won't have to climb the stairs to get Katie. Not that I would have to if I was Grand High Overseer of the World. I'd just hire a flunky to do that for me.)

4. During school holidays, parents must go to bed by eight thirty at night (nine if they've been good), and all children under sixteen get to stay up as long as they like. Also, it will be against the law for parents to wake kids up before noon.

I'm sure there will be more to add.

SNUFFLES WATCH: Snuffles still sleeping off his out-of-cage adventure. He hasn't moved much at all since he came back.

MONDAY, DECEMBER 30

9:00 a.m. Snuffles is dead!

I knew something was wrong when I opened the cage to feed him and he didn't try to gnaw my finger off. He was lying still beneath all the sawdust, and when I moved him I saw there was a huge lump on his stomach. That must have been what killed him.

He was stiff, but he couldn't have been dead long, because the Zombie Police hadn't arrived to collect him, and they usually come within the hour.

I felt really horrible about the poor thing. I'd only had him a few days, but still. I should have been nicer to him. I mean, the poor guy died all alone, just a few feet away from me.

I'll admit this here, although I'm not sure I should. I cried a bit. And it wasn't because I was scared of getting into trouble. I cried because I felt really bad for him.

10:00 a.m. Still no sign of the Zombie Police. Has there been a spate of hamster deaths that they're busy attending to? Some kind of hamster plague? I checked the news channels, but there was no mention of anything strange going on.

11:00 a.m. Getting worried. They should have been here by now. Snuffles's lifechip must have transmitted his death signal ages ago.

12:00 noon They still haven't come. Definitely something odd going on. Went to ask Dad where Snuffles's paperwork was. Said I wanted to keep it safe. He said it was in the kitchen drawer. I winced. Our kitchen drawers are like bottomless pits, filled with dangerous implements no one knows the use for, string that has wrapped around everything in the drawer, Scotch tape that is sticking to everything else, and various other things that no one wants to throw away because they're convinced they might need them at some point in the future. (They never will.)

When I finally found the certificates I noticed from the address that the pet shop Dad bought Snuffles from was in a very seedy part of town.

I phoned the pet shop, and a recording kicked in after a few rings: "This shop has been closed down by order of the Zombie Police due to failure to comply with proper pet-handling legislation. Any customers who bought anything from this location are ordered to report to their local detainment facility immediately. Seriously. Like, right now."

There was a brief pause, then the voice continued.

"Um . . . I know that sounded a bit heavy and intense, and you're probably thinking 'No way I'm reporting anywhere,' but I promise, nothing will happen to you. Seriously, I promise, and I don't even have my fingers crossed. So just head on over to the detainment facility and we'll say no more about it."

I slammed the phone down and decided to confront Dad.

A look of panic flashed across his face, and he pushed me out into the backyard.

"Not so loud! Your mom will hear!"

I asked him why that was a problem.

"Because she told me to get the hamster from the mall. You know, the big one in the center of town."

"But you didn't?"

"I didn't have time! It was Christmas Eve!"

"So . . . what were you doing?" I asked. "You were gone all day."

Dad lowered his head and mumbled something.

"What?"

"I said there was a back-to-back retrospective of the original *Star Wars* movies showing downtown! How could I pass up a chance to see them on the big screen again?"

Ah. *Star Wars*. That explained everything. My dad is a bit obsessed with those movies. To be fair, they are really good movies, and he'd passed on this love to me and Katie. (We didn't have much choice, really. He used to watch all of them at *least* once a week. We grew up with them.)

Although I have to say we don't hold the same hatred he does for "the other three movies."

"Just the originals?" I asked. "Not the prequels?"

Dad's face turned cold. "Wash your mouth out with soap, son. Haven't I raised you better than that?"

Yeah. *Star Wars*. Completely obsessed with them. But only the originals. Mention anything after *Return of the Jedi* and he gets a bit crazy. I tried to get him to watch *Clone Wars* one day, and he gave me this sad, disappointed look and left the room.

"Sorry," I said. "So . . . Snuffles?"

"There was a pet shop just outside the movie theater. I got him there." He frowned at me. "Why all the interest?"

"Um . . . no reason. Bye."

I sprinted back to my room. That explained everything. The Zombie Police hadn't come because the hamster probably didn't even have a lifechip inserted.

I sat down on my bed and pondered the situation. No lifechip meant no Zombie Police. That was something. But how to explain that to Mom? If I told her Snuffles was dead, she'd figure out what Dad had done, and he'd be in big trouble. Plus, they'd both think I couldn't look after a hamster.

Maybe I could just take care of it myself?

Bury Snuffles in the backyard and tell everyone he escaped? Hmm. That had possibilities. I'd get into a bit of trouble for letting him escape, but it wouldn't be too bad.

I heard a strange scuffling sound and looked up.

Snuffles was standing in his cage doorway. Staring at me.

I'd been wrong! He'd just been sleeping after all.

But then I saw that the huge growth on his stomach had burst or something, revealing his tiny rib cage.

I froze for a second while the truth hit me. I didn't want to accept it at first, but as I stared at the poor creature in front of me there was no denying it.

Snuffles had become a zombie!

A zombie hamster.

I had no idea what to do. Nothing in my life had in any way prepared me for a zombie hamster giving me the evil eye.

He was watching me intensely. His eyes were no longer shiny and black. They were now dull and grayish. His mouth was opening and closing, almost as if he was eating something.

What to do?

Destroy it, said a voice in my head. *You have to take it out.*

Yes. Destroy it. Good idea. Stop the infection from spreading. I looked around my room for a suitable weapon. The only thing within reach was *The Lord of the Rings*, the big hardcover version with the cool Alan Lee paintings. I hesitated. Did I really want zombie hamster splattered all over Tolkien?

But there was no other option. I reached slowly across to my bedside table. Snuffles's head moved jerkily, following my movements. I picked the book up, hefting its weight. It should do the job.

I slowly stood up and approached the cage. Then I encountered a second problem.

How was I supposed to do it? Snuffles was standing on the lip of the cage entrance. If I just whacked the cage, I might not even hit Snuffles. I needed to get him out onto the table.

I tried nudging the cage with my foot, but it just slid across the table. Snuffles didn't budge from his position. Just rode the cage like he was standing on a boat.

I tried again, and at that instant my door swung

open and Mom came in with my laundry.

I panicked and accidentally kicked the cage off the table. It tumbled onto the floor, sending Snuffles sailing through the air like an undead superhero hamster. He landed in the hallway, did a somersault on the carpet, then scurried away toward the stairs.

I'll say one thing for zombie hamsters. They don't move as slowly as their human counterparts.

"Matt!" shouted Mom. "What are you doing?"

"Snuffles!" I gasped, shoving past her.

Snuffles had curled up and was rolling down the stairs like a bouncing ball. I raced after him.

He bolted along the hall. Dad was carrying a huge pile of firewood inside, so the front door was wide open. I tried to get ahead of Snuffles to slam it shut, but I tripped on one of the stupid throw rugs Mom insists on leaving everywhere and landed on my stomach.

I pushed myself to my knees just in time to see Snuffles dart through the door and out into the front yard.

Was it my imagination, or did I hear a little undead squeak of triumph as he did so?

TUESDAY, DECEMBER 31

8:00 a.m. Right. Two things on the agenda today. First off, search for Anti-Snuffles (as I dubbed the new, evil version of my pet). And second, avoid the preparations for our New Year's Eve party. It's become something of a tradition over the years. A tradition to try to throw a good party, and a tradition to fail. Miserably.

My parents like to think it's everyone else's fault, but there comes a time (like, after the sixth year running) that you have to shoulder the burden of blame yourself.

If past parties are anything to go by, the sequence of events will be as follows:

1. Awkward beginning where no one really talks to one another.
2. Dad will play really bad '80s and '90s music.
3. An argument will start about something that happened twenty years ago.
4. Someone will say something bad about *Star Wars*, and Dad will get into a huge argument.
5. Someone (most likely Dad) will sing "Danny Boy" very loudly and very badly.
6. The end.

There are usually slight variations to the theme, but that's only window dressing, something to keep everyone guessing. Like the time Uncle Stuart and Aunt Bev were on a trial separation, and Aunt Bev brought her new boyfriend to the party. He was fifteen years younger than she was. Uncle Stuart challenged him to a duel outside on the lawn, and the police had to be called in.

9:00 a.m. Uncle Stuart and Aunt Bev have arrived. Ten hours early! Mom is freaking out in the kitchen while Uncle Stuart and Aunt Bev sit at the dining room table. Aunt Bev is in power-saving mode, staring blankly out the window. Uncle Stuart is reading an old romance novel.

10:00 a.m. Dad brought the folding table in from the garage and started going through his CD collection. Dad is DJ every year, despite all our attempts to stop him. I think he looks forward to it. A few hours of power, where his decisions hold sway over tens of people. I tried to speak to him about entertaining Uncle Stuart (his brother), but he was singing something about it being "Safe to Dance," so I just let it go.

11:00 a.m. I spent most of the day checking the yard and house for Anti-Snuffles.

List of Protective Gear

1. Hockey mask.
2. Towels wrapped around my arms.
3. Dad's leather gloves.
4. Mom's boots that go all the way up to her knees. On me they go all the way up to midthigh, which is perfect

※ *39* ※

zombie-hunting protection.

5. Metal TV dinner tray strapped to my chest.

6. Second metal TV dinner tray strapped to my back.

7. One old butterfly net.

I looked at myself in the mirror, then decided it wasn't enough, so I put on Dad's padded winter jacket as well.

The weight was a bit much. I tipped slowly over onto my back and rocked there like an upturned turtle. I kicked my legs, but it was no good. I couldn't get up again. Had to call Mom. She helped me up, looked at my getup (paying close attention to her boots), and asked me if there was anything I wanted to talk about.

When I told her I was hunting zombies she looked relieved and said good luck.

No sign of Anti-Snuffles anywhere. Very worrying. What should I do? If I tell the Zombie Police, Dad will get into trouble. But I can't just leave a deadbeat hamster running around Edenvale. Who knows what will happen? Nothing good, that's for sure.

8:00 p.m. Party off to a good start. Healthy turn-out. I helped Mom scrape the burned part off the bottom of the appetizers, so at least there's food. Charlie, Aren, and Calvin arrived at seven. Calvin just stood by the chips, stuffing one after another into his mouth. He would have done that all night if Mom hadn't slapped his hand and moved him away.

9:00 p.m. Horror! Dad decided to take to the dance floor.

My dad is . . . not a good dancer. You realize that's an understatement? It's like saying zombies like to eat brains. Have you ever seen a toddler trying to jump? They clench their little fists, bend their knees, screw up their faces in concentration, then try to make the leap. They launch, they jerk up, but their feet stay glued to the floor.

That's how Dad dances. He picks a spot and doesn't budge from it, dancing in his strange, jerky bounce with a fierce look of concentration on his face.

And pity the poor fool who tries to change the music while Dad's away from his DJ table. His normal, easygoing gaze turns on anyone going within two feet of our old CD player and freezes them on the spot. He doesn't stop bouncing, just turns his head and shoots invisible hate rays from his eyes until the offender backs away from the music.

1:00 a.m. Party went off without a hitch. Everyone surprised. Especially Mom. She floated around the house congratulating herself on a great party. I understand why she did it, but it must have looked a bit self-absorbed to those who didn't know our history of terrible events. Even Dad's rendition of "Danny Boy" got a smattering of polite applause. Everyone's gone home now. Time for sleep.

WEDNESDAY, JANUARY 1
New Year's Day

I couldn't be bothered writing this last night because I was too exhausted after the party, but as I was closing my curtains to get ready for bed I saw a movement in the yard below. I opened the window and leaned out into the cold air, trying to see what had caught my attention.

Then I saw him.

Anti-Snuffles.

He was sitting in the middle of the lawn, basking in the glow of the streetlight. Staring at me. Seriously. He was staring directly at me. If he'd had fingers he'd have been doing that pointing-at-his-own-eyes-then-pointing-at-me thing. You know, the one that means "I'm watching you."

I grabbed the butterfly net and ran downstairs, but by the time I opened the front door he'd vanished.

Seriously worried about this. Was he coming for me? Did turning into a zombie hamster give him some sort of superintelligence? Was he the world's first zombie hamster supervillain?

THURSDAY, JANUARY 2

I e-mailed Charlie and told her to come over. I couldn't keep this a secret any longer.

"So let me get this straight," she said, after I'd explained it to her. "Your dad bought you a hamster from a sleazy store, and now it's turned into a zombie?"

"Yes!"

"And it's escaped?"

"Yes!"

"And you called it Snuffles?" she asked, trying not to laugh.

"I didn't call it Snuffles! The name sort of came with the hamster. But now he's called"—I paused dramatically—"Anti-Snuffles."

Charlie frowned at me. "Auntie Snuffles? That's a weird name for a zombie hamster."

"Not 'Auntie' as in a relative. 'Anti' as in the opposite of. The evil version."

"Got it. Well, I like the name Auntie Snuffles. Was the hamster a boy or a girl?"

"I have no idea."

"A girl, I think. Auntie Snuffles, the zombie hamster. It has a nice ring to it."

"It's Anti-Snuffles!" I protested. I mean, come on. It's kind of hard to be freaked out by a hamster called Auntie Snuffles.

"Do you want my help?" Charlie asked.

"Well, obviously," I said. "Why else would I call you over?"

"Then what's her name?" asked Charlie pointedly.

I sighed. "Auntie Snuffles," I mumbled.

"Good," said Charlie brightly. "Now, let's see if we can find her and release her into the wild."

I should point out here that Charlie is a bit of an activist, even though, in my opinion, she sometimes gets a bit confused about what she's being an activist *for.* She's currently a member of the Undead Liberation Front, a group of students campaigning to allow deadbeats to roam around outside the walled cities and live their own lives without interference from us. Free from Zee-Zees and that kind of stuff. When I tried to point out to her that it was hard to give zombies their freedom when all they really wanted to do was leap for your throat, she told me it was an *internal* liberation.

Then she punched me in the arm.

We put on our deadbeat defense uniforms. Charlie had a hockey goalkeeper outfit. I was a bit jealous of that, especially when I pulled on my mom's boots and Charlie laughed and headed out into the backyard.

We spent ages searching for any sign of Anti-Snuffles (I refuse to call him Auntie Snuffles), but couldn't find anything. I even got my Sherlock Holmes magnifying glass to check for footprints, but the ground was frozen solid.

Charlie eventually got bored and went home to play Runespell against Calvin and Aren.

FRIDAY, JANUARY 3

Had to come up with a plan. I couldn't let Mom or Dad find out about Snuffles. I mean, that's obvious. First, I'd get into trouble because I let the hamster die, even though it wasn't my fault, and second, Dad would get into serious trouble (from Mom and from the authorities) for buying a pet without the proper paperwork. So I took Katie to the local Toys Я Us. (I had to take her with me. What if I'd been spotted buying what I wanted to buy? My already shaky street cred would have gone up in smoke.)

Of course, getting Katie there in the first place wasn't exactly easy. When I went upstairs to ask her, she was playing with her Cally and Edward dolls, the ones she got for Christmas, pushing them in Cally's pink car. But as I watched she rammed the car full speed into her new dollhouse. Cally's head flew from her shoulders, and an explosion of red burst from the headless doll, splattering up everywhere. Tomato sauce. I hoped.

Edward was flung from the car as well. Katie made him crawl across the carpet and propped him up against the dollhouse with Cally's plastic head in his lap.

"Oh, Cally," said Katie in her Edward voice, "this is all my fault. If only I had a brain instead of good looks, I would have told you to put your safety belt on. But my brain is the size of a walnut, and now all I've got left is your head."

Katie then put on her Cally voice. "Oh, Edward. Did you realize that the human brain can still function for up to three minutes after decapitation? Kiss me, my love. Let my last sight be your beautiful but stupid lips."

She then switched to her Edward voice again. "Eew, gross, Cally. Anyway, I was bringing you here to break up with you. I'm seeing your sister Sally. So this all worked out really well for me. Ha-ha-ha."

Cally voice: "Foiled again! It serves me right for not paying attention in school and relying on my good looks to get me through life. If only—*eurgh*."

Edward voice: "Good. Now she is dead. Perhaps a bear will eat her, and I won't even have to bother with a funeral."

It was at this point I closed my wide-open mouth and interrupted her, asking her to come with me. She agreed, but only if I bought her a Wednesday Addams doll.

A small price to pay to keep from being found out, I'm sure you'll agree.

So I've kept up the suspense long enough. I bet you're wondering what I bought. I went down there planning on buying a small remote-control dog, or a hamster or a guinea pig. Anything that I could bury in the sawdust and activate whenever Mom came near. My thinking was that I could move it around in the sawdust so she thought he was still alive.

I found something even better. Okay, it's a kitten, but a kitten that activates whenever someone comes close to it. Some kind of infrared sensor or something. I had to take out its voice box, though, seeing as it meowed and purred every time you walked past it.

(Katie walked in on me doing that. A knife poised above the toy's throat. She stared at me for a while, then nodded and said, "I approve, big brother. Carry on.")

But it's all set up perfectly now. I've put the cage in the corner of my room, by the top of my bed. No one needs to go near there for anything. If Mom does venture up that way, Snuffles 2.0 will wriggle around a bit beneath the sawdust, looking like a real, living hamster.

It's even brown, just like Snuffles 1.0.

SATURDAY, JANUARY 4

10.00 a.m. Had a visit from the Neighborhood Communications Officer. She was a tall, thin woman with her hair tied up so tight it pulled her face back as if she was standing in a gale-force wind. Every time she talked, the tension made her hairline shiver and tremble. I kept expecting her hair to burst free from its bindings, erupting into a huge, bushy halo, while her face sagged back into its natural wrinkles and lines.

"Is your mother/father/caregiver or nanny in?" she asked when I answered the door.

I thought about this. "Yes, yes, no, and no."

She frowned slightly. At least she tried to, but the only outward appearance was a tiny line appearing in the center of her forehead.

"May I speak with one of them?"

I thought back to the last time I had seen my parents. Mom had been standing in front of our faulty oven, scolding it hysterically and trying to stop it from popping open, and Dad had been trying to do something he called the moonwalk instead of writing like he was supposed to be doing.

"They're a bit busy," I said. "Can I take a message?"

"I suppose so. But make sure you tell them, yes? Failure to pass on a message from a designated NCO can result in a fine and/or imprisonment. Do you understand?"

I nodded.

"Good. Message is as follows: All families are to report to the town green tomorrow at eleven a.m. sharp, when there will be an important government announcement. Good day to you, child."

10:30 p.m. As I was drifting off I suddenly realized I had forgotten to tell Mom and Dad about the meeting on the town green. Will cook them breakfast before I break the news. That should soften them up.

SUNDAY, JANUARY 5

Plan failed. Mom and Dad in miserable mood. Sure, I forgot all about it and only remembered to tell them with twenty minutes to go, but is that any reason to get upset?

Freezing cold today. Our breath misted before us as we all waited outside city hall. Vendors were selling hot chocolate and coffee, and my freezing hands were wrapped around a cup of boiling brown water while I tried to stamp the circulation back into my feet. I couldn't tell if I got the coffee or hot chocolate. It tasted terrible either way.

The doors of city hall finally opened. The mayor stepped out, blinking in the bright winter sunlight, clutching Pugsley to his chest.

But no one paid any attention to him. Everyone's attention was focused on the man emerging behind him.

He was about six feet tall. His dark skin and long leather jacket stood out against the snow-draped buildings and trees. The mayor opened his mouth to speak, but the man stepped in front of him and surveyed us all with a penetrating stare. I couldn't help feeling he looked vaguely familiar.

"Hey," said Dad. "That's—"

He didn't get a chance to finish, because the man put his hands on his hips and started speaking.

"My name," he called out, "is Kilgore Dallas. And before anyone asks, yes, that's my real name. I had it legally changed." His voice was deep and booming. It resonated around the square outside city hall. "Some of you may recognize me from the movies I used to make before I retired from acting to become a full-time zombie hunter. But I want you to know that was a different life." He flashed a bright smile. "That's right. I'm Kilgore Dallas, and I'll be your new head warden."

This caused a wave of impressed murmuring to sweep through the crowd. Since the formation of the Zombie Squads, every town now also had a head warden, an experienced zombie hunter whose responsibility it was to educate and protect the town in case of an attack.

Our previous head warden was Old Man Ebenezer, who, despite his name, wasn't actually a villain from a *Scooby-Doo* cartoon. It was about time he was replaced, though. He was about a hundred years old or something. The zombies were in better shape than Old Man Ebenezer.

"Now I just want you to know that I don't think I'm better than any of you because I can obliterate a zombie's head at thirty feet while simultaneously wielding a bowie knife with my teeth. And make no mistake, I can do that. I lived with a wolf pack in Siberia. I became a member of their pack. They taught me their wolfy ways." He gave us a long stare. "The reason I'm better than you is a combination of genetics, intelligence, and charisma." He cracked a smile. "Plus I'm easy on the eyes. Am I lying, ladies?"

An old man standing next to me leaned down to whisper in my ear. "He's not lying, sonny. That's as fine a specimen of a man as you're ever likely to see."

"This town has become lazy," continued Dallas. "Soft. Your security is a joke. You need to toughen up, and I'm the man who's going to make sure that happens." He swept us all with a fierce look. "And I know there's one person here who agrees with me. Thomas Hunter? Where are you?"

Thomas Hunter? *Dad?* What did Kilgore Dallas want with Dad?

Judging by the sudden sickly color of his face, Dad didn't know, either.

"What have you done now, Tom?" whispered Mom.

Dad shrugged helplessly and slowly raised his hand. Dallas zeroed in on him immediately.

"There he is. My man in Edenvale. Give that man a round of applause. Come on. *Do it!*" Dallas waited until the hesitant applause had died away. "Never in the twenty years the Zombie Zappers have been in use have I heard a better voice track. Honest! Truthful! None of this poetry garbage! None of this whining about dead relatives. Just pure, honest, gutsy tell-it-like-it-is. You, sir, are the man."

I tried to shrink down into my shoulders. Dallas had obviously heard about the Zee-Zee recordings and thought Dad did them.

"Okay, listen up. There are some changes I'm going to make over the next few months, but the first thing I want to do is make sure you guys are prepared in the event of a zombie invasion. To that end, it's now compulsory for all citizens, male and female, over the age of ten to participate in zombie preparation drills. What that means is, I'll lead you outside the wall, and we'll hunt us some zombies." He raised his hands in the air. "And before all you parents start freaking out about your kids, just don't. Okay? Just don't. I'll be there, and I'll protect them with my life. No stinkin' deadbeat is going to take one of Edenvale's kids. Not on my watch!"

A burst of spontaneous applause broke out.

"Now, any questions?"

Dad raised his hand. So did quite a few others. Dallas pointed at Dad.

"Hunter. Shoot."

"Uh, I was wondering . . . what was in the briefcase? You know, from *Pulp*—"

"I can't say."

"Oh." My dad paused. "Do you still have your lightsaber?"

Kilgore Dallas's smile became a bit forced. He looked at all the raised hands.

"Any questions *not* relating to movies I've been in?"

All the hands went down.

"Then we're finished here. Have a good day, citizens."

MONDAY, JANUARY 6

1:00 p.m. Charlie had come up with a plan regarding Anti-Snuffles.

"We need to speak to Old Man Ebenezer," she said. "See if he has any tips for us. You know. Like how to trap zombies and stuff."

Remember when I said before that Old Man Ebenezer wasn't a *Scooby-Doo* villain? Well, that was true, but he does look like one.

When we knocked on his door, he yanked it open immediately, as if he had been waiting there. His white hair stuck up from his head, looking like he'd just had an electric shock. He scanned the street behind us, then stared at us suspiciously.

"Breathe onto this," he ordered, thrusting a small mirror at us.

Charlie looked at me. I shrugged and breathed on the mirror. Charlie did the same, and only after checking that our breath had misted on it did the old man relax a bit.

"Have to be sure," he said. "Don't trust the new warden to keep out deadbeats. Now, what do you want?"

We told him we were doing a school project and needed advice on hunting and trapping zombies.

He told us to wait, then disappeared inside for about ten minutes. He came back and handed us a piece of paper, then muttered something about meddling kids and slammed the door on us.

We headed back home, reading the paper as we walked.

Old Man Ebenezer's Top 10 Deadbeat Dos and Don'ts

1. Run away. Best thing you can do. Only an idiot tries to fight a deadbeat.
2. If you can't run away, aim for the head. Best piece of advice I can give. Always aim

for the head. If you're too short, aim
for the legs, then aim for the head.
3. Be quiet. Seriously. Something about
   becoming a zombie makes the critters'
   hearing better than normal. They can hear
   a whimper of fear at a hundred paces.
4. Never go in blind. Always have an exit
   strategy, an escape route.
5. Go up high. Ever seen a zombie climb a
   tree? Or a wall, or anything like that? No.
   'Cause they can't.
6. Buy some good running shoes. And make
   sure whoever you're traveling with doesn't
   have as good a pair as yours, 'cause if the
   zombies are coming you really want to
   be able to outrun everyone. I know that
   sounds ruthless, but it's survival of the
   fittest.
7. Deadbeats are really stupid. Seriously.
   Stupid, stupid, stupid. Best thing to do if
   you're being chased is to lure them into a
   room and lock the door. They'll eventually
   just fall to pieces.
8. Never turn your back on a door. Deadbeats

have a very good sense of dramatic timing, and if you turn your back on a door, that's when a zombie will come through it. A subpoint to this is never, ever, ever, ever stand in front of a window. Just don't.

9. If anyone says "I think we're safe now," or "I think we're going to be okay," or "I think the worst of it is over," or any similar-sounding phrase, run away very quickly from that person. As mentioned in point 8, zombies have a great sense of drama and will probably wait for someone to say something like that before launching an attack.

10. Finally, if, for whatever reason, you want to trap a zombie, pick someone you don't like, tie them up somewhere, and shout and scream as loud as you can.

Then run.

"I can't help feeling he didn't really think that last point through," said Charlie. "There's no mention of how we actually catch a deadbeat once it turns up."

"The basic idea is sound, though."

"What, we find someone we don't like and tie them up in your yard?"

My thoughts turned briefly to Aaron Miller, the class bully. But I'd probably get in trouble for that.

Instead, I shook my head. "We adapt it. I've got an idea."

8:00 p.m. Charlie has gone home now, but not before we prepared our trap for Anti-Snuffles. It consisted of a raw steak from the freezer (Dad is not going to be happy when he finds it missing), a heavy wooden box propped up with a stick, a short length of string pushed through the steak and tied to this stick, and one really old iPhone found in Dad's office.

Charlie and I recorded ourselves talking on the iPhone, and I pushed play and turned the volume up just loud enough for Anti-Snuffles to hear. Then we put it beneath the crate. Hopefully he'll come before the battery runs out.

TUESDAY, JANUARY 7

7:00 a.m. Anti-Snuffles is toying with me. I know that now.

I went down to check on my trap and saw that it had been sprung. The stick had been yanked, and the box was down. I threw my sack over the whole lot, then yanked it up.

I heard the iPhone knocking on the wood, but that was about it. No enraged squeaks and squeals.

I carefully opened the sack to check and saw that Anti-Snuffles wasn't there.

But the steak was gone.

And, even stranger, the iPhone wasn't playing anymore. It was recording instead. I moved the slider back to the beginning and pressed play.

I expected to hear Charlie's voice and mine coming out of the tiny speaker, but I didn't. I heard something much worse.

The zombified squeaks of Anti-Snuffles.

A cold chill ran through me. What was he saying? Was it some kind of zombie rodent warning?

I looked around warily, and as I did so, I caught a glimpse of beady eyes in the flower bed. Then there was a rustle of leaves and they were gone. I went to check and saw tiny footprints in the snow.

The problem was, there wasn't just one pair of footprints, but quite a few. And of different sizes.

I swallowed nervously and retreated inside.

Anti-Snuffles had made this personal.

7:30 a.m. A letter came for me. I don't often get snail mail, so I was really excited. Perhaps a distant relative had died and left me a massive fortune.

I looked around the cluttered kitchen, at Mom glaring as she sipped her second cup of coffee (it takes a while for Mom to warm up in the morning), at Dad muttering under his breath while he practiced his villain speech for the chapter he was going to write today, at Katie staring at me and not blinking. (She's like a snake.)

"So long, suckers," I muttered, ripping my letter open. As soon as I laid my hands on my newfound wealth I'd be out of here, living it up in a mansion. I'd have twenty butlers, ten for me and the other ten to buttle for the butlers. That's how cool a boss I'd be.

List of Amazing Things I'll Buy with My Money

1. Swimming pool filled with Jell-O. Obviously, it would have to be changed every few days, but I'll be rich, so that's fine.
2. Finance my own movie. I'll hire Steven Spielberg or Peter Jackson to be an assistant director. That way I can watch them and learn without their thinking I don't know what I'm doing.
3. A movie theater in my bedroom. Or maybe a bedroom inside a movie theater. I'll decide later.

Unfortunately, it wasn't a letter informing me of my newfound wealth. It was from the head warden's office. The seventh grade is going to be the first to take part in the Outdoor Acclimatization Program with Kilgore Dallas. I'm instructed to pack my tent, buy some supplies, and report to the city gates on January 18.

So I'm not a millionaire.

But hunting zombies in the wild should be interesting.

Plus, it means I'll get away from Anti-Snuffles for a few days.

2:00 p.m. Tricked! What a cop-out. When Mom read the letter, the first thing she did was phone the warden's office to protest what she saw as a dangerous and pointless exercise.

Trust Mom to try to ruin all our fun.

Except it turns out it wasn't going to be that much fun anyway. It was all a trick.

We were never going to be in real danger. Dallas was taking us out into an area of the forest that was fenced off. (Although we weren't supposed to know that.) Plus, he had guards stationed in trees all around the perimeter, just in case any deadbeats came too close.

Apparently, he was going to get a few of his men to dress up as zombies and give us a fright. Then he was going to demonstrate the correct way of taking out a zombie. The fear and danger of this event was supposed to sear itself into our brain and, Dallas's theory went, from that moment on we would instinctively know how to act if we were ever attacked.

Adults are weird.

WEDNESDAY, JANUARY 8

3:00 p.m. Scandal in Edenvale! (If I don't make it as a movie screenwriter/director then I should become a journalist. I'm always interested in what's going on in the world around us. I told this to Charlie and she just snorted and said there was a difference between sniffing out a good story and being nosy. Whatever.)

Anyway, here's the news. Our teacher, Mr. Craston, has run off into the wild.

I heard Mom and Dad talking about it in the kitchen. Apparently, he went a bit crazy in the head, talking about how aliens were trying to control his mind and how he needed to be one with nature. He ran through the streets with a tinfoil hat on his head and used a homemade grappling hook to climb the wall, shouting that he was Batman. Then he ran off into the forest saying he was going to bring justice to the wild.

I knew we were a tough class to teach, but that's a bit extreme!

2:00 a.m. Right. Am back in bed. That was . . . well, it was terrifying, frankly. That's what it was.

I'll explain. I was playing some Runespell earlier tonight. (With my headphones on. It was way past lights-out, and if Mom knew she'd kill me.)

Charlie, Calvin, and Aren were playing as well. We'd formed an adventurers' guild in the game, and we were currently trying to raise money to buy an inn.

I had my back to the window. The moon was bright, and I hadn't closed my curtains.

I sensed something moving on the wall above my computer. I glanced up and saw a huge shadow, a ravening beast with jaws wide open and clawed hands ready to strike.

Look, I'm not ashamed to say it—well, I am, really, but you would do the same—I shrieked.

I whirled around, but there was no ten-foot-tall

monster standing on my windowsill. In fact, there was nothing.

I moved slowly over to the window and peered out. The moon was high in the night sky, shining through the huge birch tree in our front yard. I squinted until I finally spotted what had caused the shadow.

Anti-Snuffles.

He was moving slowly along the tree branches, arms out in front of him like a human deadbeat. It was his shadow that played across my wall, stretched out and grotesque.

I looked farther along the branch and saw an owl perched in the tree. It hadn't heard Anti-Snuffles, and the zombie hamster was only a few feet away.

I opened the window, and the noise startled the owl. It looked quickly around, saw Anti-Snuffles, gave an angry hoot, then took quickly to the air.

Anti-Snuffles whirled around to face me.

If this was an old '70s movie, the camera would do a fast zoom toward his face at this point, taking in his angry glare, his snarling mouth, his evil eyes.

He chattered at me, and it sounded like he was telling me off.

Then he jumped from the high tree branch and did a belly flop in the snow. He lay there for a few long moments, then got to his feet, gave himself a little shake, and headed off along the sidewalk.

But he wasn't getting away again.

I dashed back to my computer, pulled up a chat window, and typed, "Snuffles sighted. Get bikes and meet me on the corner." I'd already told Calvin and Aren what had happened with Snuffles, so they knew what I was talking about.

I pulled on my clothes and slipped out into the hallway. I could hear Dad mumbling away to himself in his office along the hall. (I say office, but it's a converted laundry room. Tiny.)

I snuck downstairs, then went through the kitchen, and out the side door into the garage. I grabbed my BMX and headed toward the street. As I got to the sidewalk, Charlie shot out of her drive, almost crashing into me. Up ahead, I saw Aren and Calvin pulling out of their driveways as well. It's handy, all of us living on the same street, especially when we need to meet in the middle of the night to chase zombie hamsters.

Charlie and I veered out onto the road and

pedaled hard. We lived in a quiet neighborhood, so there was no danger of cars. Aren and Calvin rode out to join us.

"Where is he?" asked Aren, moving close so I could hear him.

I had been wondering that very thing. Finally, I saw a flash of movement off to our left. Sure enough, Anti-Snuffles was running into a side street.

"There!"

We swerved into the street to follow. Anti-Snuffles glanced back and chirped angrily at us. He was really fast for a dead hamster. He darted around the side of a house, forcing us to pedal faster and come back onto the street from the other side.

We caught sight of him dashing across the road.

"He's heading for the park!" shouted Charlie.

We put as much speed into it as we could. The cold wind buffeted my face as we flashed past the metal gates and pedaled along the empty sidewalks.

He led us on a good chase, I'll give him that, drawing us beyond the park and into the woods. He was using the trees now, leaping from trunk to trunk, branch to branch, a little shadow that vanished briefly only to reappear farther ahead.

The moon shone down through the spindly branches, so bright it cast shadows.

We lost sight of Anti-Snuffles about five minutes later.

We skidded to a halt in a small clearing. The trees hemmed us in on all sides.

"Any sign of him?" asked Aren.

"You'll know when I see him," said Calvin. "Because I'll definitely be screaming."

I swallowed nervously. In the infamous words of Han Solo, I had a bad feeling about this.

Charlie spotted the squirrel first. It popped its head around a tree trunk and stared at us. At least, I think it stared at us. It was in shadow, so it was kind of hard to see. But a second later another head appeared, then another, and another.

I looked slowly around to see hundreds of squirrels staring down at us, still and silent.

"Are they—are they all *deadbeats*?" whispered Charlie.

I studied the squirrels with growing horror. The stillness, the glinting of moonlight on tiny eyes. Were they? Were we about to be attacked by a horde of deadbeat squirrels? What an embarrassing way to go.

There was a scuffling of leaves. We all turned to see Anti-Snuffles approaching along the path, his shadow stretching ahead of him as he came closer.

"Guys?" whispered Calvin. "Shouldn't we leave? Like, really quickly?"

"I think Calvin has a point," said Aren, his voice shaking slightly. "A very good point, actually."

I looked at Charlie. She looked back.

Then we screamed and yanked our bikes around, pedaling faster than any of us had ever pedaled in our lives.

Everyone peeled off into their driveways as we drew level with their houses. I was the last, riding on my own along the street. I stashed my bike, ran as quietly as I could up the stairs, and jumped beneath the covers of my bed, making sure not a single piece of my body was exposed.

Scary.

THURSDAY, JANUARY 9

It's been eleven days since the creation of Anti-Snuffles, and after the events of last night I realized that things are escalating. Anti-Snuffles isn't content to just live out his life as a deadbeat hamster. No, he's turning other creatures. And not just squirrels, it seems. (As if hordes of deadbeat squirrels isn't terrifying enough.)

I saw this newspaper article today.

MISSING PETS MYSTERY

Residents of Edenvale are growing more and more concerned about household pets mysteriously vanishing.

"My little Snookums was only out in the yard for two minutes," said Mrs. Wilson, 64, "and when I went outside again he was gone. Vamoosed."

Many pets have disappeared. Anonymous police sources say tiny footprints have been found in the snow at the scenes of the incidents.

———

There was more, but I had read enough. It's pretty clear what's happening: Anti-Snuffles! He has become my nemesis. My Lex Luthor. My Joker. And it's getting serious. If he's recruiting other pets to his little army, we're going to have an outbreak of animal zombieitis inside the walls of Edenvale.

And guess who'll get the blame for that?

I have to put a stop to it.

But how? I have no idea where Anti-Snuffles is. In the park somewhere? I don't think so, because people walk through the woods during the day. He'd be spotted. No, he has to be somewhere else.

I needed to get the gang together, because these types of things are best done in groups. The Hardy Boys. Harry Potter and his friends. The Famous Five.

What can we call ourselves? The Famous Four? No. Too similar. The *Furious* Four? Sounds a bit angry. The Fantastic Four? No. Don't want to get sued.

The Four Stooges? (No.) The Four Musketeers? The Four Amigos? The Magnificent Four? What about losing the number altogether?

The Eradicators. Hmm. That's not bad. I'm sure Charlie will have a problem with it, though. She'll say it's too violent or something, which is a bit rich coming from someone so handy with her fists.

FRIDAY, JANUARY 10

Got the gang to come around. Spent an hour arguing over names. Charlie has made a list of possibles. Her number one choice is the Liberators. She also suggested the Fabulous Four and the Illuminators.

Terrible, all of them.

Calvin suggested Mystery Inc. But again, we had to explain to him about being sued.

It was eventually decided to put the issue aside for a while. Until we could come up with a better method of voting. One that wasn't decided by Charlie glaring at us and casually balling her hand into a fist.

SATURDAY, JANUARY 11

My life is officially over. And for a change it doesn't have anything to do with Anti-Snuffles.

I found out who Mr. Craston's replacement is going to be at school.

Mom!

She's always been a substitute who comes in every once in a while to cover for sick teachers. But this is long term. For the rest of the school year. That means months and months of having Mom as my teacher.

I asked her if I could transfer to a different school, but she told me to stop being so melodramatic.

This is the worst news in the entire history of the world!

SUNDAY, JANUARY 12

Last day of vacation. Such a depressing time. Even when you get an extra week like we did (the school was being repaired after the gymnasium roof collapsed), it's never enough. It feels like when your favorite show is getting canceled, or you hear the local cineplex won't be getting *Death Planet 5: The Return of the Parasites*. (I'm still broken up about that. Charlie and I had this really elaborate plan to sneak in and watch it. We'd heard it was the most violent movie ever made.)

List of Chores Before Going Back to School

1. Schoolbag packed.

2. Trip to supermarket to buy things for lunch. As usual, Mom favored so-called "healthy" snacks instead of the sugary treats us schoolkids really need to get through the school day.

3. Frantic reading of the assigned book we were supposed to read during the holidays. I don't know why they don't assign us good books. Like *Star Wars* tie-ins. Or *Harry Potter.* Something like that. No. Instead we have to read the classics, which just means lots of heavy, boring text with no humor or action scenes.

   They call it Literature. With a capital *L*. And what is it good for? Nothing, that's what.

All that's left is to mope around wondering where all the time has gone. It seemed like only yesterday we were taking off from school, the whole glorious Christmas break stretching ahead of us, filled with so much potential.

And I'm no closer to catching Anti-Snuffles. I was really hoping to solve the problem before school started, but there's no chance of that now.

I even took a ride out to the woods, which was an incredibly brave thing for me to do, especially considering what happened the other night.

But there were no deadbeat squirrels. No Anti-Snuffles. In fact, the whole forest was strangely quiet. I mean, sure, it's the middle of winter, but you expect to see a few lone animals. Maybe a bird or something.

Nothing. Not a thing.

How can no one have noticed this yet? Are adults so blind to the world around them?

MONDAY, JANUARY 13

So. First day back at school. It went as badly as I thought it would.

Class with Mom was pretty intense, let me tell you. All the kids knew she was my mom, so they were all waiting to see who had the power.

See, that's the thing. It's not just about Mom teaching my class. I have my cred (such as it is) to think about. If I let Mom boss me around, then I'll be a mama's boy for the rest of the year. So I had to assert my dominance from the beginning.

I was pretty terrified. Mom's not someone you want angry at you. But I had no choice. She'd forced my hand by accepting the teaching post.

First thing in a new school year, or when a new

teacher starts: find your seats. Here's something I learned last year. If you want to sit at the back, don't pick a seat at the back. I did, and the first thing Mr. Craston did was order the whole back row to switch with the front row. Guess he figured all the troublemakers would be trying to hide at the back, so he wanted them where he could keep an eye on them.

So this year I sat in the front row. Dead center. Right in front of Mom's desk. Back straight. Eager smile on my face. It was a gamble, but I was sure it would pay off. Well, sort of sure. Actually, I was *hoping* it would pay off. Otherwise I'd be stuck there for months.

But it worked. She entered the class—and it's an odd feeling seeing your parents out in the real world. You usually just see them at home, where they're supposed to spend their life looking after you, cleaning up after you, feeding you, that kind of thing. To actually see them interacting with the outside world feels a bit like watching one of those nature documentaries.

And here we have the long-legged mammal, the Homo sapiens motherus. *It is very rare to see a* Homo sapiens parentus *outside of its natural habitat, the family home. See how unsure this* Homo sapiens motherus *is of her surroundings, how her clumsy hands find it difficult to interact with normal, everyday objects like desk chairs and whiteboards.*

Mom was dressed in a smart shirt and dress pants. Where did she get those? I only ever saw her in jeans and T-shirts. Okay, fine. On occasion she puts a bit of effort in and uses some makeup. Maybe wears a blouse or something. But these were professional clothes. Business clothes.

She put her briefcase down on the desk and looked over the class. I could see she wasn't happy with me sitting there grinning at her. (Which was part of the plan.)

She did what I knew she would do.

"Those of you sitting at the back, please swap with everyone at the front."

Groans and complaints greeted this, but Mom knew the score. Let us get away with anything now, and we'd think we could do what we wanted for the rest of the year. So she slammed her hand down hard on the desk. The crack echoed through the class, silencing everyone instantly.

"*Now,* please."

With a few grumbles, we all swapped seats. I leaned back and put my hands behind my head. I had picked the chair behind Stefan, the biggest kid in the class. He says he's got a glandular problem. Whatever. All I cared about was that he was big enough to shield me from Mom's view.

Achievement unlocked: class ninja.

TUESDAY, JANUARY 14

Charlie decided our group should be called the Illuminators. I let her think she got her own way, but secretly I know we're really called the Eradicators.

Our first move was to go and interview Mrs. Wilson about the disappearance of her cat.

It took a while for us to actually make her understand what we were doing there. I blame old age. I mean, she must be about fifty. She thought we were there to shovel snow from her drive.

"You want to what?" she asked us.

"We want to examine your yard," I explained for the fourth time. "To see if we can find any clues about your cat, Mr. Tiddles."

"Snookums," she corrected.

"That's what I meant. Of course. Snookums. What did the police say?"

"The police? The police didn't come."

"You see?" I said, looking at the others. "What did I say? No one takes these disappearances seriously. It's a crying shame," I added, shaking my head and thinking back to the detective show I watched with Dad the other night.

"You—you think the police should have come? I thought that, too, but my daughter said we would be wasting their time."

"Some people just don't understand the pain of losing a pet, ma'am."

At this point, Charlie was snorting and snuffling, trying to stifle her laughter. Aren was smiling slightly, and Calvin was just looking confused.

"Is—is your friend all right?" asked Mrs. Wilson.

"I'm afraid we just don't know," I replied, glaring at Charlie. "Her parents dropped her on the head when she was a baby. Repeatedly."

"Oh, what a shame. She does look a bit . . . you know . . . funny."

Charlie stopped snorting and straightened up.

I knew she was probably about to say something incredibly rude and offensive, so I quickly stepped in front of her.

"The thing is, Mrs. Wilson, we're actually searching for other missing pets in the neighborhood as well." (True, by the way. Not a lie.) "We'd really like to take a look to see if we can spot anything."

"Well, okay then. Come on."

She led us around the side of the house and into the backyard. A wooden fence surrounded it. A small lawn in the middle and flower beds around the edges.

"She was over there," said Mrs. Wilson, pointing to a mound of earth against the back fence. "It's where she does her . . . business."

We headed over to the . . . well, the poo graveyard, really. (What? That's what it was.)

"What do you expect to find here?" asked Charlie.

"Yes, the odds of anything remaining are—well, they're pretty low," said Aren. "I could work them out exactly based on the weather, snow cover, rain, and average temperature, but it might take a few minutes."

"Don't tell me the odds," I said in a gruff voice.

"Was that supposed to be Han Solo?" asked Charlie. "Because it isn't."

I ignored this baseless attack on my impersonating skills and studied the fence behind the spot where the cat went to the toilet.

"Look."

There was a hole at the bottom of the fence. We all got down to study it and found some hair stuck to the edges.

"Aha!" I said triumphantly.

"That proves nothing," said Charlie grudgingly.

"Why are we here?" said Calvin, looking around in confusion. "I think someone promised me ice cream."

We climbed over the fence to the street on the other side. We checked the sidewalk, and sure enough there were little dark spots on the ground.

Blood.

We followed the trail all the way to a storm drain in the side of the road. The metal grating that covered it was loose, so I lifted it and peered into the huge floodwater pipes. They really were massive. I reckoned we could walk along them without having to bend over much. I hung my head through the hole and looked both ways. There was more blood on the walls. I could see lots of tiny footprints in the mud and sludge that had collected in the drain. There could be only one conclusion.

I straightened up and faced the others. "Anti-Snuffles has an underground lair," I said in awe. "And he's creating an army of deadbeat pets."

"This hamster is, like, the *coolest* zombie *ever*," said Charlie with glee.

WEDNESDAY, JANUARY 15

Had a bit of a standoff with Mom today in school. I knew it was coming. After I defeated her in the War of the Seats, she had to respond. She had no choice.

See, here's the thing. We both have everything to gain and everything to lose. If I let the class see me acting any differently from how I normally act, they'll call me a mama's boy. And if Mom lets me get away with anything, then everyone will say it's unfair and I'm getting special treatment.

So I decided to kill two birds with one stone.

I got up early (which shows you how committed I was) and headed into school before Mom got there. I then superglued everything on her desk.

Everything. The pens, the pencils, her stapler, her desk calendar, the apple that was there from yesterday. *Everything.*

She wasn't happy when lessons started, I'll tell you that. She tried to lift her pen. Then another pen. She stopped moving for a bit then, and the rest of the class could sense something was happening. She briefly prodded a few other items, then leaned over her desk and stared at the class.

"Who," she said calmly, "has superglued my belongings to my desk?"

No one said anything. There were a few gasps, a few sideways looks. This was big. This was serious.

"Let me rephrase that," said Mom. "Someone has superglued my belongings to my desk. If the person doesn't own up, the entire class will get detention. For a week."

There. Exactly as I thought it would happen. I waited to let the tension build (hey, I'm a bit of a showman), then I loudly scraped back my seat and stood up.

Mom locked eyes with me. I could sense the class looking at me in wonder and (I think) awe.

"Do you have something to say, Matthew?"

"It was me."

More gasps. This was like a courtroom drama on TV. All heads swiveled to face Mom. Her mouth set in a firm line and she nodded.

"Fine. Report to the principal. And you've got detention." She paused here for effect. I must have inherited my showman skills from her. "For a month."

Gasps of horror from everyone. A *month*! That was simply unheard of. The record for the longest detention goes to Lowbrow McNee. This was before my time, but it has entered into school legend. He found boxes and boxes of industrial-strength gelatin. It was out of date or something, thrown away by Jell-O makers. And during the course of one night he threw all of it into the school swimming pool. Needless to say, the sight of divers bouncing and skimming along the wobbly surface of the pool was something that would always be remembered. And McNee had to own up. You couldn't do that kind of thing and not take responsibility. He spent the rest of his school career as one of the cool kids.

He got three days' suspension and two weeks' detention.

So as you can see, I'm a bit ahead of him here.

I trudged out of the class, and only when I was in the corridor did I smile. I had done it. Now no one could call me a mama's boy or a teacher's pet, and Mom gets to look tough because she sentenced her own son to a month's detention.

Everyone wins.

Well, except for the fact that I had a month of detention ahead of me.

Still, I *think* it was worth it.

THURSDAY, JANUARY 16

I've been noticing a lot more lost pet signs stuck to lampposts around town. So many, in fact, that they've started to overlap.

We're talking the whole range of animals here. Lost cats. Lost dogs. Lost guinea pigs. A lost chinchilla. (I don't even know what they are.) A lost pig. (Who had a pig? Honestly, that's insane. And why hadn't I heard about it before now?) Lost snakes. Lost mice. Lost rats. A lost chameleon. Even lost fish. I had to read that one twice, but it was legit. Someone who said her fish had gone missing was offering a reward for their return.

What was Anti-Snuffles's plan? Was he just acting on instinct, or was it something more evil?

FRIDAY, JANUARY 17

11:00 a.m. The missing pet scandal has finally hit the big league, which means my time is running out.

See, for the past five years, the mayor has organized a Best Pet competition for the whole town to take part in. And every year the scale of the event has gotten bigger and bigger. It's not just the competition. It's a daylong event, with a minicircus, rides for the kids, live bands, food stalls, and games.

And every year, guess who wins?

If you guessed the mayor and Pugsley, the wall-eyed pug, you'd be absolutely right.

It's not as if the voting's rigged or anything, just that everyone knows whose dog it is and no one wants to make the mayor angry.

Of course, if he were a decent person, he wouldn't even take part. But he's not. He's an idiot with a wig so bad it looks like an animal is living on his head. (The prize for best pet should go to his wig.) Anyway, the point is he's announced a reward for anyone who has information about the missing pets. He's under the impression that it has something to do with the competition, that someone is trying to ruin his yearly moment of glory where he takes a victory lap around the park in front of city hall in his golf cart while his aide holds up Pugsley for all to see, like that scene from the beginning of *The Lion King*.

The pet competition takes place at the beginning of next month, so that means I've got a couple of weeks to deal with it. Despite the Zombie Police being staffed by cavemen, they do have advanced equipment back at their headquarters. So if they find the missing pets before we do, it's possible they can trace them back to Patient Zero: the first of the pets to turn deadbeat.

Which means it could come back to me.

And to Dad.

10:30 p.m. Aargh! Tomorrow is our Outdoor Acclimatization Program. I completely forgot about it! They want us to be at the city gates at *six*. In the *morning*. That's just . . . inhuman.

11:45 p.m. Can't sleep. Keep thinking about how early I have to get up tomorrow.

12:34 a.m. Why do you torture me so, mind? You know I need to get up in a few hours. Why are you keeping me awake?

1:43 a.m. This is beyond a joke now. I wonder if someone slipped me some coffee at suppertime.

2:24 a.m. Should I just give up? Just get up, maybe put in some hours on Runespell? Or catch up on some reading?

3:37 a.m. Eyes feel like they are too big for my head. And raspy. I can hear them moving in my skull.

Tomorrow—*today*—is *not* going to be fun.

SATURDAY, JANUARY 18

8:00 p.m. So here we are, at the end of our first day of camping. (Or the Zombie Acclimatization Program, as Dallas informed us it was now called—ZAP! for short. Not bad. Dallas claims he came up with it himself. Which is fine. Even though it does clash with my own acronyms for the Zee-Zees.)

Anyway, we're all alive and well. A bit cold, but it *is* winter, after all. And Dallas made sure we all had these portable heaters and luxury tents and everything. We've even got a huge fire going in the middle of the campsite, with all the tents circled around it.

It's not that bad, actually. I don't know why Dad

always said camping was so terrible. Admittedly, the stories he told about his times in the woods were quite worrying. I wasn't sure if it was the wet seeping up through the floor of the tent, the wind that cut through the material and stopped you from getting to sleep, or the snakes, or the bears, or the mosquitoes. I think it was just a combination of all of the above, to be honest, and every time I brought up camping he always had a new story to tell about how horrible it was.

Now that I look back on it, I reckon Dad was just too lazy and made all that stuff up. Unless he and Granddad were the unluckiest campers in the entire history of the world.

But I should fill you in on everything.

The day started at five in the morning.

I'll just pause here and let you absorb that. *Five* in the *morning.* I didn't even know such a time existed.

I moaned and groaned when the alarm went off, partly because I had only fallen asleep about an hour previously. I pretended to be unconscious, but my dad eventually stumbled into the room, pulled my duvet off, grabbed my foot, and dragged me onto the floor.

"Your mom says to get up," he mumbled, and then he picked the duvet up and collapsed onto my bed, curling up and going right back to sleep.

I don't think Mom is used to being up so early, either, because she gave me a mug of coffee. I drank it down, thinking she had done it on purpose to give me a boost. It tasted horrible. At least, it did to start with. But my mom likes a lot of sugar in her drinks, so the sweetness soon got rid of the taste, and it actually wasn't that bad.

A few minutes later my teeth were chattering. And not from the cold. My heart was thumping heavily in my chest. I was convinced I was having a heart attack. I couldn't keep still. My arms were twitching slightly, and my head felt like it was doing somersaults.

The school bus arrived a few minutes later. Mom gave me a long hug and told me to stay with Dallas at all times, and at the first sign of trouble I was to climb up a tree and wait. I reminded her that the whole thing was a pointless sham anyway, but she still told me to be careful.

I was the last pickup, so I had to sit at the front of the bus, right behind the driver. Aren, Charlie, and Calvin all sat a couple of rows behind me.

The driver smelled of garlic. He *always* smelled of garlic. I think he keeps it in his pocket or something. The word around school is that he's afraid of vampires. (I hesitate to put this in the journal, but here it is: there have been a few news reports lately about sightings of vampires and werewolves.)

Seriously.

Not here, but farther north, and over in Europe, which is, like, pretty far away. Aren also told me his family had heard rumors of these weird vampires in North Africa. His parents seemed to think they were real, but come on. What are the chances of us having zombies *and* vampires *and* werewolves existing in the real world?

The bus soon arrived at the town gates. We filed out to find Dallas already waiting for us, along with three men and two women, all of them dressed in camouflage gear. They were driving those open-top jeeps you always see in movies, the kind that usually have machine guns attached to the back. (And this despite the freezing weather. Looking cool is hard work.)

These didn't have machine guns, although Calvin swore he saw one hidden in the back under some tarp. But Calvin sees a lot of things. Hears a lot of things as well. So we never know when to believe him. We've all just decided it's best to disbelieve everything. It's easier that way.

Dallas was standing by the wall. He typed a combination into an electronic keypad, and the huge gates shuddered and started opening outward, drifts of snow falling to the ground.

"Right!" he shouted. "You kids awake?"

There were a few mumbles.

"I *said*, are you kids awake!?" he shouted.

"Yes!"

"I'm not," muttered Charlie. "I think this could be considered cruel and unusual punishment in most states."

"Good," said Dallas. "Now, what we're going to do is extremely dangerous. You understand? Extremely dangerous. The only thing stopping you kids from being the main course on a deadbeat buffet is me and my team. Say hello, team."

The team didn't say hello. They did chew gum at us, though. I wished I had some gum.

"I need you all to listen to me very carefully. You are to stay close to us at all times. Don't ever stray away from the group. You'll all be given one of these." He held up some kind of portable siren. "If you get lost, you climb a tree and you turn this on. You can all climb trees, can't you? You're kids. That's what kids do."

Everyone turned to stare at Calvin. He wasn't exactly the best of athletes. None of us were, actually, except for Brad Johnson. And he wasn't even here. But I was sure Calvin would manage to climb a tree if he was being chased by a horde of zombies.

He looked quite worried, so I patted him on the shoulder.

"Don't worry, Calvin. Just stick with us."

He nodded, but he was starting to get that panicky look that usually sets him off doing something stupid. I leaned in close.

"Remember, none of this is actually real," I whispered. "It's a trick. Remember I told you?"

His face collapsed into grateful relief. By now all of us kids knew this was a setup. That we were never going to be in any real danger. But Dallas and his crew had gone to a lot of effort, so we all agreed to go along with it. It would be cruel not to.

Even so, it was slightly creepy to walk between those gates and out into the snow-covered field.

The Zee-Zees were switched off at night, and there weren't any zombies around, so it's not as if we were in any danger. But still, leaving those walls behind, the walls that had protected us our entire lives—I admit to feeling a tiny flutter of fear. (Just a tiny flutter.)

'Course, it was worse when we got to the woods. Mom had explained that there was some serious fencing around the area we were being led to. We couldn't see it, though, so it felt like we were walking straight into the zombies' home turf.

"Nobody step on a twig," whispered Dallas.

Just as he said this, Calvin stepped on a huge stick. The crack echoed around the forest like a fart in a church.

He flushed red. "Sorry."

We walked for about forty minutes. The sky was beginning to lighten when Dallas and his crew finally led us into a clearing about twenty yards wide.

"This is where we're going to camp," he said. He nodded to his crew, and they all disappeared into the trees.

"They'll keep the perimeter clear," said Dallas. "But there is a chance they'll all get taken down, so we're going to set up a secondary perimeter here at the camp."

For the rest of the morning the forest clearing rang with the tweets and chirps of messages coming and going on everyone's phones. We were supposed to be surviving in the wild, but I guess no one told the cell phone companies that. Everyone in our group was in touch with their homes, sending worried parents pictures of our camp, of each other, of Calvin falling face-first into the snow. The usual.

Dallas eventually got so fed up with us staring at our phones that he confiscated all of them, sealing them in a plastic case.

"You'll get them back after you've been one with nature," he said.

The rest of the day was mind-numbingly boring. Chopping wood, lighting fires, cooking bacon and eggs, putting the tents up, that kind of thing. I mean, if this is what it was like in the old days, I have no idea how my parents survived. They're always telling me they didn't have the Internet back then. Or cable, or computer games. I mean, what did they actually do with themselves? I enjoy reading as much as my dad, but even I would get bored with that if it was the only entertainment I had.

Most of us were pretty annoyed with Dallas for taking our phones, so we kind of gave him a hard time. Every time we did something we thought might attract zombies (if this was real, which it wasn't) we would ask Dallas if it was safe. When he said it was, we'd ask him why, and his explanations were becoming more and more exasperated.

"Because they don't like the smell of bacon!" he shouted.

"*Everyone* likes the smell of bacon," I pointed out. "Even vegans like the smell of bacon."

"No, they don't. And even if they did, so what? Zombies don't. Zombies like fresh meat." That was all we had for amusement, and even that got boring. To be honest, I wasn't even sure why we were here. Dallas says it's to teach us about life beyond the wall, but none of us ever goes beyond the wall, so what was the point? And the whole deadbeat attack thing? Another waste of time. It's not as if we're going to be given dangerous weapons or anything like that. The whole thing was fake.

We all turned in as soon as night fell, thinking that the quicker we went to sleep, the quicker it would all be over.

SUNDAY, JANUARY 19

9:00 a.m. So. First night slept in the wild.

How was it? I hear you ask. Well, it was pretty uncomfortable, thank you. The ground was lumpy no matter what position I tried to lie in. It was freezing cold despite our portable heaters, and Calvin, we all discovered, talked in his sleep. Really talked. Full-on conversations with someone called Binky.

We asked him the next morning who Binky was, and he looked confused and said the only Binky he knew of was Binky the clown, the mass-murdering children's entertainer in a horror novel he swiped from his dad's room.

I thought back to some of those conversations we overheard.

"I can't do it," Calvin had said. "Binky, don't make me. They're my friends."

And "What hammer, Binky? You put one in my bag? Why would you do that?"

And, of course, how could I forget, "Who's annoying you, Binky? Matt?" A pause, while Calvin must have been listening to his dear friend Binky, the murderous clown. "How can you even suggest that, Binky? I couldn't do that!"

Needless to say, we've all been a lot nicer to Calvin today.

He's been smiling a lot, though, which leads me to suspect some foul play. But I really don't think it's worth the risk finding out the truth, do you?

11:00 a.m. We've all been wondering when Dallas was going to try to scare us with his "deadbeat attack." He told us that today we were going to learn about "defensive circles," "minimizing our footprint," and other things that sounded like incredibly hard work. But we all assumed this is when his crew (who we hadn't seen since they left the camp yesterday) would stumble into our midst doing their best zombie impersonations.

In the meantime, Dallas was having a bit of

a hard time with our families back in Edenvale. When he confiscated all our phones yesterday, our updates to our families suddenly went silent. All at the same time.

You can imagine what they thought had happened. Dallas's phone, which he only switched on this morning, has been bombarded with increasingly worried and then panicked calls from our parents.

Dallas gave our phones back in disgust, and ten seconds later all twenty of us were seated in a circle around the fire, heads bowed, updating our social networks and letting our families know we hadn't been devoured by deadbeats.

Hmm. *Devoured by Deadbeats*. Cool name for a movie. Must remember that.

Anyway, it was while we all had our heads down that the "attack" came.

None of us noticed at first. I was checking out the movie sites, trying to find news on the latest *Star Wars* films. Charlie was on my right. She told me she was getting in touch with her comrades in the Undead Liberation Front, but I saw her phone. She was reading up on celebrity gossip. Calvin was playing Tetris, and Aren was actually catching up on his homework. I'm not kidding. That guy is an overachiever of note. If he's not careful he's going to overheat his brain. Kids our age aren't meant to do that amount of work. Scientific fact.

So anyway, I was just about to click on a juicy bit of info about who was going to play the young Han Solo when I heard a low moan behind me.

I glanced over my shoulder and saw that a "deadbeat" had entered the camp and was shuffling directly toward us.

How typical! Dallas launches into his fake lesson just when he gives us our phones back! I wonder if he thought this was symbolic of something.

Well, I for one wasn't going to be distracted. He was going to take our phones away again in ten minutes. It wasn't fair of him to try to distract us now.

There was another moan from up ahead. A second deadbeat had entered the camp. I gave this one more than a quick look, because even I had to admit they'd done a good job with the makeup. It looked as if half its face had rotted away. Bone and sinew showed through the skin on its arms.

Not bad. Not bad at all. I swiped my finger across my phone screen, held it up, and took a photo.

None of the others had noticed yet. I nudged Charlie and nodded toward the zombies. She looked up and frowned.

"No," she said. "No way. He's only just given us our phones."

You see? Me and Charlie, we're on the same wavelength. That's why we're best buds.

More of Dallas's crew, dressed up in zombie makeup, shuffled out of the trees. I remember thinking there were more fake zombies than there should be, but I just figured Dallas had more people hiding out in the forest and roped them in to scare us.

It wasn't working, though. We were all too engrossed in our phones. Heads bowed, concentrating, while a circle of deadbeats slowly closed in on us, groaning and moaning.

One of the deadbeats got close and grabbed Charlie's arm. She was yanked backward off her log, crying out in surprise. I whirled around and saw that this guy was really taking this joke thing seriously and was about to clamp his teeth down on Charlie's hand.

That's when I noticed a few different things. First, I could see through the guy's rib cage. Like, actually see right through it. He was between Charlie and me, but I could see her angry face through the yellowing bones. He had no skin, no internal organs.

My brain did a few rapid recalculations of the situation just as Kilgore Dallas entered the clearing, returning from his angry walk. He froze, a look of utter astonishment on his face.

That's when I realized this wasn't a joke. This was a real deadbeat attack.

I shouted a warning to everyone and lunged forward, shoving the deadbeat who was about to bite down on Charlie. Its grip was so tight, and my shove so hard, its arm ripped right out of the socket. I looked at Charlie in horror. The zombie arm was still attached to her wrist. She shook her hand, but the thing wouldn't let go.

She got to her feet just as another deadbeat arrived.

Charlie then used the arm that was clamped around her wrist as a makeshift club, smacking it against the deadbeat who was stumbling toward her. It was one of the coolest things I've ever seen.

The zombie spun in a circle and fell to the

ground. Charlie yanked the arm off and threw it away.

Dallas was now running through the camp with a baseball bat.

"Up the trees!" he shouted. "Remember the drill!"

The others had finally twigged that this wasn't a joke. That it was the real thing. They were scrambling for the trees, dodging around the slow-moving deadbeats, and pulling each other up through the branches to safety.

Except for Calvin.

He was engrossed in his game and taking no notice of all the commotion. Charlie, Aren, and I were already climbing an old, twisted oak tree, but we saw him sitting there and shared a look. Then we sighed, dropped back to the snow, and sprinted toward him.

Aren grabbed his phone, Charlie slapped him on the head, and I pulled him to his feet.

"Hey!" he shouted. "What's the big idea . . ."

He trailed off as the situation finally sank into his brain.

By this time, Dallas's crew had arrived. They and Dallas were running around the clearing dealing with the deadbeats in violent and fascinating ways. Our classmates were peering down from the branches, those who still had their phones using them to record the events. Deadbeats were still stumbling around, searching for anything with a pulse.

That included us.

Three were heading in our direction. We ran back to our tree and helped Calvin up into the branches. He finally made it to safety, and Charlie, Aren, and I hauled ourselves up after him. Then we turned around to watch the battle below us.

It was over in a matter of minutes.

Dallas's crew stood in the clearing, looking around at the deadbeats lying on the forest floor. None of his crew had been injured. Not a surprise. They were pretty good at what they did.

"You kids stay where you are," called Dallas. "We're going to scout around."

So we had to stay up in the trees for the next hour. Luckily for us, Aren was still holding Calvin's phone, so we all took turns playing games until Dallas came back and told us we were going home early.

So, not a totally terrible day.

MONDAY, JANUARY 20

Everyone who was on the trip is now considered something of a hero. When word got out about what happened things went a bit crazy. I thought actual steam was going to bust out of Mom's ears, she was so angry. Even Dad, who is a pretty laid-back guy, was furious. He looked at me strangely and then had to go for a walk to calm down.

I found out later that he marched to city hall and gave the mayor and Kilgore Dallas a piece of his mind. Apparently, he shouted at them. My dad never shouts.

I feel a bit bad for Dallas, though. It wasn't really his fault. It turns out that the contractors the mayor paid to put up the fence were the cheapest he could find. Plus, he didn't tell them the fence was supposed to keep deadbeats out, so they just stuck anything up, thinking it was for squirrels or something.

But nobody called out the mayor on this. Well, a few people tried, but then his offices said they didn't have time to deal with that because there were more important things to worry about. The pet crisis was getting worse, they said, and more than two hundred pets were missing. I had no idea it was so many. The mayor issued a proclamation saying that all pets were to be kept indoors until they could figure out what was going on.

I knew what was going on.

Anti-Snuffles, that's what. He had a lot to answer for.

TUESDAY, JANUARY 21

Still doing my detention at school. Mom was going to cut it back to a few days, considering what happened, but I told her not to. It made her look even tougher, and I got more sympathy from my classmates.

One of those people giving me more sympathy is Erin Deacon. She's in my class and is—well, she's, um, she's beautiful. I've liked Erin since she moved here last year. She used to live in New York City, but when the deadbeats broke through the wall around the city her parents decided to move somewhere safer.

She's really cool, knows a lot about the world, and her stories of the day the deadbeats got into

New York are amazing. The National Guard out on the streets. Running battles. Helicopters strafing the ground. It sounds like something in a Michael Bay movie.

Anyway, she passed me a note after class broke up. It said, "I think you're really brave. XX."

XX. Hmm. Is that vague or not? I mean, it's not definitive, is it? She might sign all her notes like that. And she didn't say "I think you're amazingly good looking," or even "I think you're cute." No, it was "I think you're brave."

Is she just being nice? I don't have anyone I can ask. Nobody knows I like Erin. I can't tell Charlie. She'll just make fun of me. Calvin—well, I'm not even sure he knows the female species exists. There's Aren, but I once heard him talking about how love was nothing more than a—let me see if I can remember—a "biological imperative, a chemical command meant to ensure the future of the species."

Yeah, I'm not sure any of them would understand.

WEDNESDAY, JANUARY 22

2:30 p.m. Charlie wasn't at school today, so I stopped at her place on the way home.

She was huddled on the couch beneath a blanket, watching reruns of *Friends* on TV. She didn't look good. She was really pale and sweating.

"What happened to you?"

"No idea," she said. "Must have caught something out in the nature." She said the words "the nature" as if it was something alien and evil.

"Shouldn't you see a doctor?"

"I'm going tomorrow."

"Okay. Well, I'll see you around. No offense, but you look really sick, and I don't want to catch whatever it is."

"Thanks, buddy."

"No worries," I said, then hurried home.

3:00 a.m. Well, that was interesting. I was asleep earlier tonight when I got a text message from Charlie.

"On roof. Need company."

I got out of bed and slid the window up, leaning as far out as possible where I could just see Charlie's house. Their garage was attached to the side of their house, and Charlie was sitting on its roof, wrapped in a thick blanket. She saw me and waved.

I ducked back in and threw on some clothes, then dragged my own blanket off my bed, sneaking downstairs and out the back door. I climbed over the fence, then hopped onto the woodshed and up onto the garage.

I sat down next to Charlie and pulled the blanket over my shoulder. She was staring up at the moon.

"How you feeling?"

"A lot better, actually."

I looked at her closely. She still looked really pale. Like, white as snow pale. She had stopped shivering, though.

"You should still go to the doctor. You look terrible."

"Gee, thanks."

And then she got a bit weird. She started talking about the old days, about our time in preschool, that kind of thing. About the time Calvin got lost in the forest and we all went out looking for him, the time we all snuck into the neighboring school and toilet-papered their basketball court. The time the four of us all went down Town Hill (that's the really steep hill in the middle of Edenvale) on our bikes, forcing all the cars to pull over, and how a police officer eventually caught us. The main thing we all remembered about this was seeing our reflections in his mirrored sunglasses as he gave us a lecture.

I wondered why she was bringing all this stuff up, but after a while it didn't matter. We were both laughing and talking about all the stupid stuff we'd done, talking about who we liked at school, who we didn't like. I even told her about Erin, and to my surprise she didn't laugh or mock me.

It was . . . nice. Despite the cold, despite how late it was, it was cool to just sit there and chat.

After a couple of hours we trailed off into silence. I looked over and saw Charlie had fallen asleep. I let her sleep for a while, but after another half hour I decided to wake her up. Lying on the cold roof couldn't be doing much for her illness.

I nudged her, but she didn't move. I had to really shake her before her eyes flickered open again. She stared at me as if she didn't know who I was.

"Charlie?" I said.

Nothing.

"Hey, Charlie. You okay?"

She didn't budge. And it was starting to freak me out, the way she was just looking at me.

"Charlie, I think you should go inside now."

She stared at me for another few seconds, then finally blinked. She looked around, confused. At the garage roof we were sitting on, at the houses around her, then finally at me.

"Matt?"

"Yes. Matt. Why do you sound so surprised?"

"I . . . I . . ." She closed her eyes. "I don't feel so good. I think I'd better get to bed."

"Sure. I'll see you tomorrow. But seriously, you need to go to a doctor. You've probably made yourself worse sitting out here."

She stood up and made her shaky way through the window that led directly into her room.

THURSDAY, JANUARY 23

8:00 p.m. Well . . . I don't know how to even begin describing today. It's been . . . hectic. I still feel sick. So much went on.

I should probably start at the beginning.

4:15 a.m. I was woken up when it was still dark by the wail of sirens outside. I leaped out of bed to see the black vans of the Zombie Squad come roaring down our street like we were in some big blockbuster movie.

I wondered why they were here.

But then I felt a sick ball of fear surge in my stomach, because the vans skidded to a stop outside my house.

My first thought was they'd found out about Snuffles. That they were coming for Dad. I was about to warn him to run when I saw the Zombie Police pile out of their vans and run, not toward my house, but to Charlie's.

I glanced to the garage roof, where we had spent our time talking before we went to bed.

And there, climbing out her bedroom window, was Charlie.

She ducked down low so the lone Zombie Squad officer waiting on the street didn't see her.

What was going on?

I hurried downstairs. My parents were up, staring out the front window, so they didn't see me as I ran out the kitchen door and got over the back fence, onto the woodshed, and up onto the garage roof.

"*Psst!*" I said. "Charlie!"

She whirled around to face me.

If I thought she looked ill earlier it was nothing compared to how she looked now. Her face was as white as the moon. Her eyes were wide and dark, filled with fear.

"Charlie. What's going on?"

"Matt," she said in a low voice. She slid along

the roof toward me. I noticed that she was holding something in her hand. Not only that, but it looked like she had a really deep cut on her forearm.

"Why is the Zombie Squad here?" I asked.

"Um . . . I think I might be in a bit of trouble."

She took my hand and placed it against the middle of her chest. I tried to pull away, but her grip was like a vise. I couldn't budge.

"What are you . . ."

My voice trailed away as I suddenly realized what I was feeling.

Or rather, what I *wasn't* feeling.

Charlie didn't have a heartbeat.

My eyes met hers, and she held up her hand. She was holding a small piece of metal about the size of a postage stamp. I recognized it immediately.

Her lifechip.

I took a hasty step back, feeling my world come crashing down around me as my brain actually made sense of what I was seeing.

Charlie was dead.

But she was still walking around. Which meant . . .

. . . Charlie was a deadbeat.

I shook my head in denial. It couldn't be. But it was. She had no heartbeat. I opened my mouth to shout for the Zombie Squad, but then I hesitated. Charlie was looking at me, her eyes filled with fear and worry. That wasn't how a zombie looked at you. They looked at you the way I look at a take-out burger a week into one of Mom's health-food kicks.

I shook my head in confusion. "What happened?" I whispered.

"Well, I'm just guessing here, Matt. And it's an *educated* guess. I think I'm dead and have somehow come back as a deadbeat, and the Zombie Squad is here to make sure I don't kill everyone in town."

"But . . . you're talking. You're . . . you're *Charlie*."

"Mmm. It's a puzzle." There was the sound of breaking doors from inside her house. "But do you think we can chat about it later, when we've gotten rid of them?"

I studied her face in the moonlight, wondering what to do. She was a zombie. A deadbeat. Every lesson I ever learned growing up, every badly made public service announcement video we'd been forced to watch was screaming at me to run away. To get as far away from Charlie as possible.

But it was surprisingly easy to ignore that voice.

Because . . . well, because it was Charlie crouching before me. I knew that. She was my best friend, and I definitely wasn't going to betray her to the Zombie Squad.

I grabbed the lifechip from her. They would use it to track her. That's why she'd taken it out.

"Wait here."

I slid back down the roof, climbed over the fence, then moved along the side of our house. (I thought I caught a glimpse of many squirrel eyes watching me from the tree outside my window, but I didn't have time to check.) I crouched down behind a bush, then darted out from cover and around to the other side of the lead Zombie Squad van. I dropped the lifechip through the window, then sneaked back around and straightened up when I got to my lawn.

"Hey!" I called.

The helmeted officer whirled around to face me. I pointed down the street.

"I just saw a deadbeat running that way. About two houses down."

The officer quickly pulled up a little monitoring device that beeped like the proximity alert thing in *Aliens*. I really hoped it only tracked the signal a few yards. Anything more precise and he'd discover my trick.

I was in luck. He held up the device, and it was pinging steadily. But then, it had been pinging steadily since they arrived at the house.

"That way?" he asked, nodding along the street.

"Yup. A real ugly one, too. All shambling and moaning." I put my arms up and shuffled across the grass to demonstrate. "I think I heard her say, 'Braaaains.'"

The officer spoke quickly into his walkie-talkie and climbed into the van. He started the engine and roared off down the street. A second later the others ran out of Charlie's house, piling into their vans. Their proximity sensors were pinging a lot slower as the lifechip drew away. They took off after the first van, leaving the street in silence once again. Hopefully they'd spend a good while chasing each other around town.

Meanwhile, I had to hide Charlie.

I turned around to find Mom and Dad standing in the door with their arms folded.

"Matt, I advise you to make the explanation you are about to give *phenomenally* good," Mom said.

I tried desperately to think of a convincing lie, but at that moment Charlie appeared and came to stand next to me. Her mom ran out of their house, saw us, and hurried over. She grabbed Charlie by the shoulders.

"What's happening?" she said, her voice tight with worry. "Why is the Zombie Squad here?"

"Well," I started to say, "it's a funny story—"

"Matt," said Charlie. "Don't."

I stopped talking. Charlie shrugged off her mom's hands and turned to face our parents. "Everyone, I've got some bad news." Then she smiled. She actually smiled. "I can't believe I'm actually saying this, but . . . I think I'm a teenage zombie."

"You're not a teenager," I pointed out.

Charlie punched me in the arm. "It's called dramatic license, you idiot. Way to ruin a moment."

6:25 a.m. Everyone crowded into our den. Mom was trying to console Charlie's mom. Dad was pacing back and forth, stopping every now and then as if he was going to say something, then shaking his head and continuing to pace.

"Genetically engineered superzombie," said Dad, stopping suddenly. "The government has been experimenting on ways to use deadbeats as controllable weapons. Charlie is part of their experiment."

"Don't be absurd," said Mom.

"No, you're right," said Dad. "The mayor doesn't have the intelligence to keep something like that hidden."

"What if she's just a new breed of zombie?" I asked.

"Hey. She's sitting right here," said Charlie.

"Sorry," I said.

Charlie reached out and took hold of her mom's hand. "Do you want to know what I think happened?"

Everyone turned to look at her.

"I think what I am—what I've become—is the normal state of a zombie. If certain . . . conditions are met. Think about it. What's the first thing any-one does if someone dies? You run. You get away as quick as you can before they come back and try to eat you. Except, when I was sick, Matt kept me company. We spent hours on the roof just . . . chat-ting about our past. I . . . I could feel it inside of me. Like who I was, was trying to slip away, but every time Matt said something, it came back again and I remembered it was me, Charlie."

We all looked at her, trying to understand her words.

"No one's ever tried that, have they?" she asked. "Everyone just thinks deadbeats are mind-less monsters. But maybe it doesn't have to be like that. If we just take the time to be there with them as they die, maybe they'll all be like me."

"When do you think it happened?" I asked.

"I think it was that deadbeat who grabbed me? Back at the camp? I checked my jacket and saw it was torn. I think he must have broken the skin, infected me. Or whatever it is they do."

"Do you feel the need to eat any of our faces?" I asked. "Because I know we're friends and every-thing, but I don't think I'd be comfortable with that."

"Relax," said Charlie. "Beyond a slight craving for some rare steak, I feel pretty good. Not tired or anything."

Huh. Who would've thought it? I'd helped discover a new breed of zombie. I wonder if they'd name it after me? Hunter's Condition. Something like that.

"But do you see how this changes everything?" said Dad suddenly. "If Charlie is a new type of zombie—sorry, Evelyn," he said to Charlie's mom, "then it's world-changing. Look at her! She's still Charlie. She's still the same. If all it takes is to stay with people as they die, if all it takes is some human compassion, then we don't have to be scared anymore."

I'd never seen Dad so worked up. But he was right. This would change the entire world. If it wasn't a fluke.

"That still doesn't tell us what we're going to do about the Zombie Squad," said Mom. "They'll be back. They'll look for her."

"We can hide her here," said Katie, who had been up since the Zombie Squad arrived. "She can sleep under my bed. Or in my closet." She looked at Charlie with a bit of a possessive smile. I could almost hear her thoughts: *My very own monster under the bed.*

"That won't be necessary, Katie," said Mom. "I'm sure we can find a mattress for her."

The Zombie Squad came back later that day. Guess they found the lifechip. They searched Charlie's house but didn't bother with us. Like I said before, they weren't the most intelligent people, and besides, who in their right mind would hide a deadbeat in their house? It was unheard of.

1:35 p.m. Mom came in to have a talk with me. She started off talking about grief and feelings of anger and resentment, guilt, that kind of thing. I was kind of puzzled, because I wasn't feeling any of that. I eventually had to stop her, and said, "Mom, you don't understand. Nothing's changed. She's still Charlie. She's still my best friend."

Then Mom started to cry and said what a good boy I was. It was a bit embarrassing, and I eventually had to call Dad in to take her away.

8:20 p.m. And here we are, all up to date. Charlie is lying on a mattress in Katie's room. I've given her a load of books to read and said she can come play games on the computer, because I don't think she's going to need sleep anymore.

I lay on my bed thinking about Mom's reaction to what I said. I wondered if I should have been scared, or disgusted, or . . . or anything. Maybe I was a freak for taking this in stride?

I thought about it for a while, then decided I wasn't a freak for accepting Charlie. Or if I was, then I was totally fine with that.

FRIDAY, JANUARY 24

7:00 a.m. Right. This is it. I'm going to fix everything this week. Before the pet competition next Saturday.

List of Things to Fix

1. Charlie. (Well, not fix her. But come up with a way for her to live among us. Which, if I'm being honest, is a tricky one.)
2. Catch Anti-Snuffles. Seriously, what happened to Charlie is huge, I know, but I have to deal with Anti-Snuffles and his zombie pet army. I just have to. Otherwise, I'm in serious trouble. And so is Dad. I don't

think I can handle having my best friend turn into a deadbeat and my dad going to jail in the same week.

3. Can't think of a number 3. Is that it? Only two things? That's not too bad, actually. I'm sure I can handle that.

Okay, possible solutions.

The Charlie Problem

1. Charlie pretends to be a long-lost twin, or a visiting cousin who looks remarkably like Charlie did. The spitting image. Maybe she can wear some big, ugly glasses to disguise her. (Hey, it works for Clark Kent.) This is necessary because she is now listed as dead by the Zombie Squad, and if she just turns up at school some rather awkward questions are going to be asked. She'll have to change her name as well. Something like Laura. Or Maddy. Something like that.

2. She'll have to wear really dark base or foundation, or whatever that skin-color makeup is that girls use.

3. Charlie invests in some industrial-grade deodorant. I'm not really sure of the processes involved, but let's face it, Charlie is a walking corpse. An intelligent and witty corpse, but a corpse nonetheless. She's going to start to smell soon.

Hmm. Actually, that's a point. Any solutions that rely on disguising who she is will only work short term. There's going to come a time when people will realize she's not quite right. That she's a bit green around the gills. Especially if body parts start to fall off.

The Anti-Snuffles Problem

1. We track the source of the storm drain, head inside with . . . with what, exactly?

Now that I'm writing this down, I'm asking myself what I am actually going to do if I *do* catch Anti-Snuffles. Looking at Charlie has turned everything around. What if he just wants a cuddle?

And then I remember those beady eyes

watching me, filled with malice. That little mouth snarling in rage.

No, Anti-Snuffles is definitely one of the old-school deadbeats. Devour brains, moan and groan, that kind of thing. So what I'm thinking is—look, I can't just kill him. I'm not like that. I know he's dead already, but still . . .

So I propose we catch him and somehow propel him out into the woods beyond the gates. I'm thinking of some form of rubber-band cannon. Just send him flying out of our lives.

And the other pets? Well, I'm kind of hoping that they follow Anti-Snuffles. Either that, or without his leadership they'll scatter through the town and the Zombie Squad can handle them. I mean, it's their job.

8:00 a.m. Charlie just gave me a heart attack. The door slammed open and there she was, her arms raised at shoulder height, her eyes blank and staring. I looked at her in horror, and she started shuffling toward me.

"Br-a-a-a-a-i-i-i-n-n-n-n-n-s-s-s-s," she moaned.

I will admit that I gave a slightly girlish shriek of fear. That was when she cracked up laughing.

"Oh my gosh!" she said. "You sound like a little girl."

"No I don't!" I squeaked. I cleared my throat. "No I don't," I repeated in a more manly voice.

"You totally do," she said, dropping onto my bed and flipping through a comic book.

I waited for my heart to calm down a bit, then stared at her curiously. "How do you feel? Any cravings for brains or living flesh?"

"No," she said with a sigh. "Nothing like that."

I couldn't help noticing she sounded the tiniest bit disappointed.

"What are we going to do, Matt? I can't hide out here forever. There's going to come a point when Dallas catches me." She straightened up on my bed. "I've been thinking about this. I reckon I should just head over the wall. Take my chances outside."

"No!" I said. "You can't do that."

"Why not? It's not as if I need food. And the other deadbeats will leave me alone now that I'm one of them."

"You're not one of them," I said firmly.

"Matt," she said, "I am. Look at me. I have no heartbeat. I'm not breathing. I'm a deadbeat."

"You're not. You're Charlie."

She opened her mouth to argue, but I held up a hand to stop her. Surprisingly, she did.

"No more. Seriously, Charlie. I'm asking you to stop."

She nodded. "Fine." Then she grinned at me. "When do we tell Aren and Calvin?"

SATURDAY, JANUARY 25

We introduced Aren and Calvin to Charlie 2.0 today. It went better than I'd expected. I mean, when Calvin finally stopped screaming and trying to climb through the wall, they realized it was still "our" Charlie, and they accepted her pretty quickly.

It was still a bit weird, though. Until Aren whipped out a magnifying glass and tried to study her skin. Charlie quickly punched him in the arm, and this put our group dynamic back to where it was meant to be. Even if Calvin does occasionally look at Charlie and whimper.

We had decided that Saturday was going to be the day we searched through the storm drains for

Anti-Snuffles's hideout. It might seem like a small problem when compared to what happened to Charlie, but the fact of the matter was that Anti-Snuffles was still out there, and we had to deal with him before he turned every single pet in town.

Today was going to be the day we ended the deadbeat pet army problem.

That's right. Today. Or possibly tomorrow. It all depended on if we actually found the storm drain. And if the pets were using it to hide out. And if we actually worked up the courage to go into the drains. And if we managed to catch Anti-Snuffles.

But soon.

We had to sneak Charlie out, because there was no way Mom and Dad would let her leave the house. But I think if they knew what we were doing they'd understand. Charlie's part of the gang. We couldn't do it without her.

We bundled Charlie into a hoodie, then we got our bikes and headed out to search for the mouth of the storm drain. I had a huge net strapped to my bike, and Aren had borrowed his mom's cat carrier. We were serious. We were going to end this.

We started at Mrs. Wilson's house, then followed the drain downhill. It took a while to explain this concept to Calvin. That even though we couldn't *see* the drain, it had to flow downward. So as long as we weren't climbing we were on the right track. I don't think he got it, but he nodded and smiled as if he did. I'd seen that look on his face in class, so I decided not to pursue the matter.

It took us about an hour, but we finally found the spot where the storm drain emptied out. It was a huge marshy area with a river running through it. Metal bars covered the hole in the wall where the river exited Edenvale and headed out into the fields beyond the town.

The wall was a bit rough here. Bricks were visible through the paint, and some bricks had actually fallen out. I noticed that Charlie was staring up at the wall.

"What are you looking at?" I asked.

"Huh?" She blinked and turned to focus on me. "Nothing." She smiled halfheartedly. "Actually, that's not true. I was just thinking that if I ever need to escape this place, if I'm in trouble, this would be the perfect place to do it. Up and over the wall in five minutes flat."

"It won't come to that," I said.

We moved through the boggy marsh to inspect

the pipe. A stream of icy water flowed out of the pipe, soaking our feet. The sound echoed back and forth inside the drain, making it impossible to hear anything else. The drain was about five feet high, so we could all fit inside. The question was, did we want to?

I flicked on my flashlight and aimed it inside. The huge pipe—more like a tunnel, really—receded into the dark.

"Well?" said Charlie. "Are we doing this or what?"

I nodded reluctantly. Everyone got their flashlights out, and I threw the net over my shoulder while Aren grabbed the cat carrier.

We entered the pipe, making our way deeper and deeper into the drain system. I was straining to hear any kind of hint that the pets were here. A squeak, a moan, anything. But the rushing water masked everything.

After a while the pipe opened into a huge square room. Water spewed from pipes high up on the walls. Metal walkways dripping with slime surrounded us.

It was actually a pretty cool location. Very moody and atmospheric.

Perfect for a horror movie.

Especially when the metal walkways were suddenly bristling with undead pets.

They appeared as if from nowhere, staring down at us, our flashlights glinting in their gray eyes. We tightened into a circle, our backs against one another, and stared at the zombie animals.

Aren looked at his cat carrier. "We're going to need a bigger cage."

Nobody moved. Not the deadbeats, and certainly not us.

"If we move very slowly," I whispered, "maybe they won't notice."

As a group we took a small shuffling step backward. The zombie animals noticed all right. They all did that "I'm so alert" thing that pets do, some of them straightening onto hind legs, others tilting their heads.

We froze. That was when I happened to look down. My flashlight was shining into the water, and I could see deadbeat fish swimming around our feet.

I swallowed nervously. Then the animals on the platform directly above and ahead of us shifted aside and Anti-Snuffles moved forward. I swear, every time we come into contact he's like a James Bond villain. I felt like shouting up at him, "Do you expect me to talk?" and he would probably reply, "No, Mr. Hunter, I expect you to *die*!"

Anti-Snuffles jumped down into the water. He was still staring directly at us as he bobbed to the surface, not once breaking eye contact. A second later he started drifting smoothly backward toward a stone ledge. I pointed my flashlight down and saw fish pushing him along.

When he reached the lip of the culvert he turned and tried to pull himself out of the water. Unfortunately, he was a bit too small and struggled to get out. He kept bobbing up and trying to grab the ledge, scrabbling on the stone, then dropping back into the water again.

Charlie let out a grunt of pity and quickly moved forward, putting her hand under his bottom and giving him a boost. We stared at her in amazement as she returned to join us.

"What?" she said. Then she seemed to realize what she'd just done. "Oh. Right. I probably should have grabbed him there? I just felt sorry for him."

I couldn't believe it! Charlie had had Anti-Snuffles

in the palm of her hand, and she let him get away.

I wondered if we could just grab him again, but when I turned my attention back, he was flanked by two of those hideously naked cats. You know, the ones with no hair? I still reckoned I could take him, but then out of the shadows two eyes suddenly glinted and a really big Rottweiler stepped forward, growling.

In fact, all the deadbeat animals were coming down off the platform, splashing into the water. Just . . . bobbing there. Watching us.

Waiting.

The Rottweiler took another step toward us. Charlie held up her finger and said, "No!" very loudly. The deadbeat dog paused, confused. It tilted its head and whined a bit, then looked to Anti-Snuffles as if for advice.

"Okay," I said. "I know that we're all wondering what the best move here is, but I'm going to suggest a course of action that involves running—"

I didn't get a chance to finish, because as soon as the word "running" had left my mouth, the others turned and bolted. Even Charlie.

I joined them, running faster than I had ever run in my entire life. The others were ahead of me, skidding and splashing through the slimy tunnels. I could hear the sounds of pursuit from behind: galloping, skittering, flapping. Every sound an animal could make as it hunted its prey was coming closer and closer.

My heart was hammering. My breath was rasping in my throat. I promised myself that after this I really would take part in some fitness program. Then I saw a circle of white up ahead. Daylight! I found an extra burst of speed and caught up with the others, all of us exploding out of the tunnel into glorious open air. We grabbed our bikes and dragged them up the hill, then climbed on and pedaled as if our lives depended on it. (Which they did.)

After we made it back to my place we collapsed on the floor in the den, wheezing, gasping, sweating. (Except for Charlie. She flopped down into the couch and looked a bit smug.)

Dad looked up from where he was writing on his iPad. "Having fun?" Then he frowned. "Hey. Your mom told me to make sure Charlie stayed inside."

"We . . . we won't tell if you don't," I wheezed.

SUNDAY, JANUARY 26

The inevitable has happened. Word has leaked that Charlie is a deadbeat and is loose in the town. The Zombie Squad is searching for her everywhere. (Led by Kilgore Dallas.) The mayor has even put out a notice saying Charlie was responsible for the missing pets.

What, does he think that she ate them or something? And never mind the fact that the pets started to go missing way before Charlie was turned.

Anyway, all animals are to be kept inside while Dallas deals with the situation. And word is he's been ordered to solve it before Saturday, when the yearly carnival and pet show is held outside city hall. Why in February, I hear you ask? My dad says it's because the town has mayoral elections shortly after and the mayor wants to make sure he gets his trophy for Pugsley in case he's not elected again. And you just know the mayor is not going to cancel that.

MONDAY, JANUARY 27

School was pretty depressing today. I kept getting these sympathetic looks because everyone knows Charlie and I were best friends.

The way I see it, Charlie actually has a pretty good deal. Sitting at home playing computer games all day and night. (She has no need to sleep, so she's already levels ahead of my character in Runespell.) Just think how cool that would be! An extra ten hours a day to do what you want. Watch movies, read comics, play games. I mean, except for the whole walking corpse thing, I don't think it would be that bad.

TUESDAY, JANUARY 28

Things are getting a bit risky. They've started house-to-house searches to find Charlie before the weekend. Mom and Dad both told Charlie not to worry, that she can hide here as long as she needs to, but I can see Charlie isn't happy. She thinks she's putting us at risk. I suppose she is, but so what? What are friends for, if not to protect you from the Zombie Squad?

Katie has been going through the house searching for a good hiding place. (She's sort of adopted Charlie as her own.) I gave her a hand, even discovering there was space between the walls. We thought this would be perfect until Aren pointed out the Zombie Squad is using sniffer dogs. I mean, I can't smell anything on Charlie (yet), but you know what dogs are like. They'd find her in a few seconds.

No one really knows what to do. I suggested taking Charlie to Dallas and the mayor and showing them both that she wasn't like the other deadbeats, that she was the first in a new breed. That when people died they didn't have to turn into brain-eating monsters. Charlie was up for it, but her mom and my parents said no.

They don't have a lot of faith in our mayor.

WEDNESDAY, JANUARY 29

11:00 p.m. I couldn't sleep, so I thought I'd ask Charlie if she wanted to play Runespell PvP online. I went to Katie's room and pushed the door open. Katie was fast asleep, *Moby-Dick* lying open on her chest.

But there was no sign of Charlie. I checked the rest of the house, but even as I did so I knew I wasn't going to find her. She'd gone. She didn't want to get us into trouble.

I wondered what to do. Wake Mom and Dad? Then what? Apparently, there was a curfew in place until the evil deadbeat had been caught. If anyone was found wandering around the city streets, he'd be arrested.

I returned to my room to think. An e-mail was waiting for me.

> From: Charlie
> To: Matt Hunter
> Subject: Good-bye
> Hey, Matt. Guess you know what this e-mail is about, huh? And don't pretend it's a surprise, because you know it's not. I couldn't just sit around and put your family in danger. I'm heading over the wall. Don't know what I'll do yet. Maybe I'll find an abandoned village or something. Maybe there are others like me out there. Not monsters. Just people who are ... changed. We know they exist. Guess it's sort of my responsibility to seek them out. I'll be a wandering Jedi, bringing peace to the recently deceased. (Or am I a Sith? It's all pretty confusing right now, to be honest.)
> Anyway, see you around.
> Charlie out.

I had an idea where she might be. Back at the wall, she'd said that would be the perfect place for her to escape if she needed to. I wasn't sure if she had been serious, but it was my only lead.

I ran out of the house and grabbed my bike,

pushing it across the lawn, checking along the road to make sure there were no Zombie Squad patrols. Then I set off.

I got to the marshlands where the pipes emptied out, and I jumped off my bike, hurrying through the boggy grass to the wall. It loomed above me, cutting the night sky in half. I looked around but couldn't see Charlie anywhere.

I was too late.

"Up here."

I looked up. Charlie was clinging about halfway up the wall. She wasn't moving. She was still wearing the hoodie, pulled up to hide her face.

"What are you doing?" I shouted.

"Got stuck," she replied. "Thought there were footholds all the way to the top. Guess I was wrong."

"Shouldn't you come down now?"

"I can't. Matt, I've got to go. The longer I stay, the more trouble your family will be in."

"I've been thinking about that," I said. (And I had.) "Let's go on the offensive."

"What, like, attack the Zombie Squad?"

"No, not attack the Zombie Squad. How would that help? I mean, we go on a PR offensive. We go to the papers. Or the news station. You go on air. You show everyone you're not like the other deadbeats. That you're still you."

"Yeah, not really sure that's going to work."

"It might! Come down and we can talk about it. It's our best bet."

There were a few moments of silence, then she sighed and started to climb back down.

She dropped the last few feet and turned to face me. "So. This plan of yours. How—"

"FREEZE!"

The voice came from behind us, making us jump at least ten feet into the air. Lights burst into blinding life, five of them glaring into our faces. I reached out and grabbed Charlie's hand.

"Do *not* move. Either of you."

I knew that voice. Kilgore Dallas. The glare of light dimmed slightly as he walked in front of the powerful flashlights and came to stand in front of us. He frowned, then looked around, appearing a bit confused.

"Names?"

"Matt Hunter."

He shifted his gaze to Charlie. "And you?"

I tightened my grip on Charlie's hand. She

responded, then lifted her head high.

"Charlie Atkinson."

Dallas frowned even more. "Is this some kind of joke? Ask me how much I like jokes."

Neither of us said anything.

"I said, ask me how much I like jokes!"

"How . . . how much do you like jokes?" we both said.

"I don't! Now I'll ask again. Name?"

Charlie released my hand, then slowly lowered the hood, revealing her white face and gray eyes to Dallas.

"My name," she said, "is Charlie Atkinson. And I'm a deadbeat." Dallas opened his mouth but paused when Charlie raised her hand in a commanding gesture. "But as you can see, I'm very obviously a new kind of deadbeat. One who has intelligence, one who can think, speak. One who has friends. Also, this is partly your fault. I got scratched when the deadbeats invaded our camp."

Dallas crouched down, staring hard at Charlie's face. He reached out slowly, gently, and put a hand against her neck.

"Now ain't this a right pain in the butt," he said. He glanced over his shoulder at the Zombie Squad still waiting behind him. None of them had lowered their weapons.

"I'm sorry, Charlie," he said. "I've got to put you under arrest."

"But you can't!" I shouted. "You can see she's normal. She's like us!"

"Kid, she's not like us. Besides, I'm doing this for her protection as much as ours." He inclined his head to indicate the Zombie Squad, who had moved closer.

"Matt," said Charlie. "It's okay. Maybe we can still do your plan?"

I looked around in desperation, seeking a way out. But there was none. Dallas was right. If Charlie tried to run now it would only end badly.

"Come on, kid," said Dallas, putting a hand on her shoulder. "My van's just up the hill."

He led Charlie off. The Zombie Squad moved aside, keeping their weapons trained on her as she passed them by. Charlie glanced over her shoulder once and gave me a small wave.

Then the night swallowed her up.

THURSDAY, JANUARY 30

When I got home last night the first thing I did was wake Mom and Dad up and tell them what happened. They went next door to give Charlie's mom the bad news.

This morning we headed over to the police station next to city hall. Me, Mom, Dad, and Charlie's mom. The police confirmed that Charlie was in one of their cells, but they refused to let us see her. When Mom started making a fuss, the police put a call through to city hall, and the mayor himself waddled on over, Pugsley the pug cradled in his arms. Dallas came in behind him. He stood at the rear of the police station, arms folded, looking really uneasy.

"I'm sorry," said the mayor to Charlie's mom. "I really am. But your daughter is a stinkin' deadbeat, no offense meant, and has thusly lost all her rights to be treated as a human being."

"But you can see she's not like the others!" shouted Mom.

"I can see no such thing. Haven't even laid eyes on the critter. Don't want to."

I looked to Dallas. "Tell him! You saw her. She's not like the others."

Dallas was silent for a moment, then unfolded his arms and nodded. "It's true. She seems to be holding on to her intelligence. Who she is. She can still think."

"That may be," said the mayor smoothly. "But it's out of my hands. Washington is sending someone on Monday to collect her. It's all signed and sealed. I'd love to help, I really would, but I'm afraid I have a pet show to organize."

He smiled a fake smile and hurried out of the police station. I saw him on the big patch of grass outside city hall, shouting at some workmen who were assembling a wooden stage.

"What are they going to do with her in Washington?" I asked Dallas.

He didn't answer. But the look on his face didn't fill me with hope.

"Can't you do anything?"

"Sorry, kid. My hands are tied."

FRIDAY, JANUARY 31

His hands are tied. Huh. Well, maybe *his* are, but mine aren't. I got Aren and Calvin and filled them in on everything that had happened. Then we spent the day coming up with a plan to bust Charlie out of prison. Aim high or go home.

Hmm. Not bad. That will be the tagline when they make this into a movie. Or, "They took his friend. He took their lives." No. Maybe not. I don't actually intend to kill anyone. "They took his friend. He . . . took her right back." No, that makes Charlie sound like a possession. Anyway, I'll sort all that out later, once I've written the screenplay.

We headed over to city hall. The small park outside was bustling with activity, so we were pretty much left alone to do our reconnaissance and sneakily film everything we could. The stage had been completed. It was even bigger than last year's. The runway where the owners walked their pets was easily thirty yards long. The mayor was making sure his time in the spotlight was as long as possible. A huge tent was also being put up. Caterers were unloading plastic tables and chairs from huge vans.

We walked nonchalantly toward the police station, then headed around the back, filming the windows and even managing to check how secure the metal guards were over the glass. (Answer: very secure.)

I checked the Dumpster that was sitting against the wall. Inside was a load of junk. I grabbed an old plastic milk crate, slammed shut the lid on the Dumpster, and steadied the crate on top. Then I climbed up and peered onto the roof. Holding my phone up, I scanned the area, then dropped back to the ground.

Sneaking Charlie out the back in a *Mission Impossible*–style escape wasn't going to be easy.

But I had a few ideas. I was sure I'd come up with a plan before tomorrow.

SATURDAY, FEBRUARY 1

6:00 a.m. I've run out of time! I've been awake all night trying to come up with a concrete plan of action. I even scoured my old books and comics to see if there were any prison breaks in them that I could copy. There were, but they all involved some form of weaponry, and that was something I didn't have access to.

It looks like we're just going to have to wing it.

What I do know is that we need some form of distraction. A big one. One that will get all the police to leave the station so we can enter and let Charlie go. I mean, most of the police will be out on security duty anyway, covering the crowds at the carnival and pet show. So it shouldn't be that hard. Should it?

Anyway, here's what I've got.

Mission Breakdown for Rescuing Charlie and Saving the Day

10:00 a.m. The day starts. Music, clowns, that kind of thing.

11:00 a.m. Meet up with Calvin and Aren. Make sure they know the plan.

12:00 noon Pet show begins. It lasts for about an hour, so that's our window. When everyone will be focused on the show. Cue distraction.

1:00 p.m. Cause distraction at police station. Rescue Charlie. Broadcast a message from her on YouTube so everyone can see she's the same as us. Just with a bit of a skin condition.

2:00 p.m. Settle in for a marathon game of Runespell with Aren, Charlie, and Calvin. The day is saved. I'm a hero.

6:00 p.m. Write screenplay of our adventures. Sell it to Steven Spielberg, Tim Burton, or Peter Jackson for a million dollars. Live carefree, happy life with servants and butlers and as much dessert as I want.

There. Not bad, huh?

10:00 a.m. I headed out to the park without Mom and Dad. They were both working with Charlie's mom to come up with a way to get Charlie out of jail, but I knew it was a lost cause. Sometimes grown-ups talk and talk when what is really needed is action.

The park outside city hall was already filled with people. These events have always been popular in the past, but this year's was the biggest ever. Music played over the loudspeakers. Kids were running around, then falling over and crying. The snow had been shoveled away from the park, but at the bottom of the rise was a frozen lake where people were skating. I could smell roasted chestnuts in the air.

Luckily, it hadn't snowed in a week. The sky was blue, so it was a pretty good day for it, despite the cold.

I was happy with the turnout. Crowds were

good for us. It meant we wouldn't be noticed.

I met up with Calvin and Aren on the steps of city hall. It was about ten thirty, so we were ahead of schedule. Calvin was eating a hot dog with one hand and sticking his face into a bag of popcorn in between bites. Aren was very carefully testing the wind with a piece of ribbon tied to a fishing rod.

"You guys get the mission breakdown?" I asked.

Aren pulled the fishing line down. "It was a bit vague."

I shrugged. "Better to stay loose."

"I think Charlie would call it making it up as you go along."

He was right. She would.

11:00 a.m. The waiting is killing me. My stomach feels like I'm about to take every single test and exam I've ever had. All in one go. And the longer we stand around, the more I start to realize that what we're doing is incredibly dangerous.

But I don't know what else to do. Charlie's our friend. We have to get her out of there. Otherwise, who knows what will happen to her?

At least the crowds are getting heavier. A few minutes ago, five policemen and three police-women left the station. I saw them wandering around and keeping an eye on the festival. That meant fewer of them inside.

11:30 a.m. The chairs around the runway and stage are filling up with people taking their positions for the highlight of the day. I take a deep breath and check on the others. Calvin was taking huge gulps from a Slush Puppy, and Aren was attaching a Velcro exercise strap around his head. It was holding his iPhone, facing outward.

"What's that for?"

"I'm filming the breakout."

"You're *what*?"

"Come on. You don't think we're going to want to look back on this day? It's going to be chaos in there. At least this way we'll have a record of how it went. Think about it. We can sell it to television networks."

Hmm. It was a good point. I wish I'd thought of it. I could use the footage for when I write the movie.

"Equal shares in the footage?" I said.

"I suppose," said Aren. Then he put his earbuds in.

I pulled them out of his ears. "What are you doing now?"

"Music. For the breakout. I saw it in a movie once. My own private soundtrack."

"Aren, I very rarely get a chance to correct you about, like, *anything*, so forgive me if I make the most of this. But are you out of your ever-living mind?"

"What?"

"You're supposed to be the smart one! If you're pumping music into your ears, how are you going to hear what's going on around you? Someone could be sneaking up right behind you and you wouldn't know. Calvin and I could be trying to talk to you and you wouldn't hear us."

I felt a bit bad. Aren looked a little depressed about the whole thing. "But I saw it in a movie."

"What movie?"

"One of the *Blade* films, I think."

I rested a hand on his shoulder. "Need I say more?"

12:00 noon Showtime. (I've always wanted to say that. Oh, and "Wait'll they get a load of me." But you take what you can get.) I turned around and clapped my hands together once to get the others' attention.

"Showtime."

Aren looked frankly ridiculous, with his iPhone strapped to his head. And Calvin was surrounded by a pile of junk-food wrappers. He looked a bit sheepish.

"Sorry. I overeat when I'm nervous."

Not the most professional crew for a breakout, but I suppose I had to make the most of what we had.

"First, pick up that litter."

We waited while Calvin took his trash to the closest bin. As he was doing this an emcee skipped up onto the stage and was warming the crowd up. I think it was Brad Johnson's dad, the local used-car salesman.

"Hi there, you beautiful people. You really are a stunning crowd. Really, I mean that. Especially you," he said, pointing and grinning at a young lady in the crowd. Someone threw an apple at his head. I stood on tiptoes and saw that it was Brad Johnson's mom.

"Ow. Okay. Well, yes. We have a lovely show for you today, we really do. Some amazing specimens, and some really weird ones—and they've brought their pets along!" He paused, waiting for applause that didn't come. "Okay, yeah, cool. Moving on. Our first contestant is a Pekingese poodle called Genghis Khan. Really?" he said to someone offstage. "Yes, Genghis Khan. Okay then. Khan the Pekingese poodle."

Calvin came back, and we hurried across to city hall and snuck inside. (It was deserted. It was a public holiday, after all. And it was a weekend. And if anything Dad says about politicians is true, then that was two more reasons than they needed not to come into work.) Each of us took a fire extinguisher from a wall. (There was one on each floor.) Then we headed back outside, skirted around the edge of the park, and headed toward the rear of the police station. The Dumpster was still where it had been. (I know you're thinking, *Why wouldn't it be?* But I'd had nightmares about this. That someone would come and move it or something.)

We retrieved the milk crate I'd found yesterday, then closed the Dumpster lid. We climbed up onto the Dumpster, tossed the three fire extinguishers onto the roof, and used the crate to boost ourselves up. We kept low and moved to the three skylights we had spotted when reviewing our footage yesterday. I glanced along the line. Calvin was grinning at me. Aren was serious but ready.

I nodded, and we pulled the skylights open. We got our wire ready, pulled the pins on the extinguishers, pushed the handles down, and quickly wrapped the wire around them to keep them open.

White smoky powder exploded from each extinguisher as we dropped them into the police station.

We scrambled down off the roof and around to the front of the station. I pulled three pairs of safety goggles and three mouth masks from my backpack, the kind painters use. I picked them up from the hardware store on the way to the carnival. We put them on, then waited for the first police officer to run outside and slipped in behind him.

The smoky powder was thick. Aren switched on the LED light on his phone, and we hurried down the corridor, avoiding the coughing and spluttering police who were staggering around.

We knew the layout well enough. We'd been here a few times in our lives. Not for breaking the law, but for school trips, that kind of thing.

We made our way to the rear of the building and into the jail. It was deserted. We hurried along the corridor, looking into each of the cells.

We reached the end and turned around in confusion.

They were all empty.

"Where's Charlie?" whispered Aren.

Very good question. Where was she?

There was a noise behind us. We whirled around. A faint whirring sound was drawing closer and closer. We watched in alarm as a white, glowing light materialized, illuminating tiny whirlwinds in the smoky powder. The light grew brighter, the noise louder, the smoke turning in twisting spirals around us.

We shrank back against the bars of the cell behind us.

A tall shadow materialized in the smoke. The minitornadoes gusted away to the sides, and the shadow moved forward to reveal—one of those little portable hand fans.

And Kilgore Dallas.

"Well, well, well. What do we have here?"

I opened my mouth. Then closed it again. Because, really, what could I say? The one thing we hadn't come up with was an excuse if we got caught.

"Um . . . we got lost?" said Aren.

"Sure you did. You got lost and accidentally ended up back here. Where your friend was being held."

"Where is she?" I asked.

Dallas was silent for a moment. "She really is different, isn't she?"

"I told you! I *said* she was."

"Keep your hair on, kid. What was I supposed to do? Surrounded by the mayor's Zombie Squad?"

"So where is she?" I asked again.

"Thing is, the mayor decided to move her. Seems your town always has one or two incidents during this . . . festival. Whatever it is. Seems your police have to lock a few rowdy souls up overnight. The mayor didn't want any of them seeing your friend."

I took a step forward. "What has he done with Charlie?"

Dallas held up a hand. "Hey, chill." He stared at me. "You dig?"

I stopped moving. "I dig."

"Good. Now, Kilgore Dallas is a good guy, you know? I signed up to protect people like you from deadbeats. That girl—she isn't a deadbeat. Least not like any *I've* ever seen. I'm not happy with her getting sent off to government labs in Washington. That's not right. Besides, we had conversations. She's a smart girl. She told me you guys' theory about why she's . . . like she is."

"And?" I asked. "Do you think we're right?"

"I think you're right." He sighed. "You realize how big this is? How she's going to change the world?"

"For the better."

"That remains to be seen."

"I think I need the toilet," said Calvin in a trembling voice.

"Where is she?" I said.

"Can't tell you that."

"But you just said—"

Dallas held his hand up again. I chilled, without him even having to ask.

"Telling you that would be breaking the law. But if I happened to be talking to you about, say, a school project or something? About city hall? About how there are old cells in the basement level? Built during the first zombie war? And that the keys for those cells happened to be hanging on a hook in the mayor's office? If I was talking about that, then I don't see it would be a problem."

There was shouting from behind Dallas. I hadn't realized, but the smoke had nearly all cleared away. Dallas glanced over his shoulder, then took out some keys, moved along the corridor, and unlocked a heavy door that led into the alley behind the station.

"Good luck," he said.

12:30 p.m. Well, that was terrifying. We stumbled outside and made our way around to the front of the building, where the cops from the station were standing around complaining about kids and their pranks.

We walked very fast around the edges of the

park, heading back toward city hall. The pet show was in full swing now. Brad Johnson's dad was still doing his thing. At least, trying to. "And now we have—well I'm not sure what this is. A mongrel, surely? Looks like a cross between a Doberman and a miniature sausage dog. Ma'am, why would you even enter that in a pet competition? It's scaring the children."

We moved behind the stage and up the steps into city hall. We'd been here last year on a school trip, so we knew where the offices were. (There aren't many places for us to go on school trips in Edenvale. The garbage dump, the police station, city hall, and the museum. We'd visited them all.)

We climbed the stairs to the second floor.

"So, is Kilgore Dallas helping us?" asked Calvin.

"'Helping' is a bit of a strong word," said Aren.

"He's . . . getting out of our way," I said. "Which is pretty much the same thing."

We found the mayor's office and headed inside. It was a big room dominated by a massive, old-fashioned desk. There was a glass candy jar right next to the mayor's computer. Calvin made a bee-line for it, helping himself to a handful.

Aren and I split up to search for the keys. Dallas had said they would be hanging on a hook. Not very secure, really, but I suppose the cells in city hall aren't actually meant to be used.

There wasn't just a single hook. There was a piece of wood with the words "You don't have to be crazy to work here, but it helps!" written along the top, and beneath these words of wisdom was a whole row of hooks filled with key rings and keys. There were at least thirty keys, maybe more.

Aren and I looked at each other, shrugged, then grabbed every set of keys and shoved them into our pockets.

We turned to Calvin. He was standing by the desk holding the jar of candy. He was looking a bit suspicious.

"What have you done?" I said.

He shook his head.

"Calvin?"

He held up his hand and shook it. His hand was stuck in the jar.

Aren and I tried to pull the jar off, but it didn't budge. I stepped back and glared at him. "Seriously?"

"Sorry," said Calvin meekly.

"Maybe we should just break it," said Aren.

We looked around for a likely surface. The edge of the desk seemed good enough. Calvin wasn't too keen, though. He squealed and turned away, shielding his face while Aren and I got ready to smash the jar against the desk.

"The glass is really thick," whispered Aren.

It was. It would take a hefty smack to break it. I was worried about cutting Calvin's hand.

"You're going to have to keep it till we get outside," I said.

Calvin brightened up. "Do I get to keep the candy?"

I was about to reply when there was a noise outside the office. We froze, ears straining.

The mayor's annoying voice could be heard, growing louder as he approached his office. He was speaking to Pugsley. (How did I know? Because he's one of those people who speak to their pets in weird baby language.)

"Just a quick little brushy-wushy and then poo-dums will be all ready to show those ugly people and their mutts just who's the prettiest dog in all the land. Yes? Yes, that's right. It is. So it is."

We panicked. I'll admit that. We ran around in aimless circles, wondering what to do. The doorknob turned. The door started to open.

We all dived beneath the desk. Yes, I know. Not very original. But what would you do?

The mayor entered his office. We could see his feet approaching beneath the desk. (He couldn't see us, though.) He was wearing one pink and one yellow sock.

He stopped in front of the desk. We heard scrabbling above our heads as he set Pugsley down. The dog was sniffing and snuffling all over the place. Then he started to growl.

"What is it, boy?"

There was a faint noise. We turned and saw that Calvin had tipped the jar up and was trying to wiggle a piece of candy out of a tiny gap. He smiled nervously and gently put the jar back down.

That was when the mayor farted. Seriously. He let rip with a huge, noisy fart. Aren gasped in horror, but luckily the noise of the fart actually drowned him out. We clamped our hands over our mouths. (Why did I pack away our masks?) Calvin forgot he had the jar stuck to his hand and banged it against his head as he tried to shield his nose. He groaned quietly.

"Pugsley!" said the Mayor in his baby voice. "Who's got a stinky bottom, hey? Pugsley does. *Yes, he does.*"

Pugsley barked, probably signaling in dog language that the mayor should keep his body odors to himself and not try to blame others.

"Now. Just a quick brushy-wushy and then we're off. I ordered a brand-new trophy, you know. Yes, I did. A big one. A *very* big one."

He was busy for a minute or so.

"There we go! All pretty and ready to win. *Yes, we are.* Yes, that's *right.*"

His feet headed back across the office to the door. Where he paused.

"What about some candy?" he said. "Should we have some candy, Pugsley? Should we?"

My breath caught in my throat. Calvin's eyes were wide with horror. We waited while the mayor decided.

"No, maybe not," he said in his baby-talking voice. "I think I can hear someone shouting outside. We should go and see what's happening, shouldn't we? Yes, we should. Besides, we've got the victory cake to eat. Don't we? Yes, we do! We do!"

He left the office.

I breathed a sigh of relief, and we slid out from beneath the desk.

"That. Was. Disgusting," said Aren.

I had to agree. I never wanted to smell anything like that again.

We hurried to the door and peered out. The corridor was empty, so we slipped out and sneaked downstairs, all the way down to the basement level. The passages here were dim. Most of the lights weren't working.

"Which way?" asked Calvin.

I shrugged. "Guess we just check every door till we find the cells."

It took longer than I thought it would. Twenty minutes at least. I thought I heard some sort of commotion from above, but I couldn't be sure, and there was no time to check. We had to find Charlie before the pet show was over.

We finally found the cells behind a door blocked by a filing cabinet. The mayor *really* wanted to make sure Charlie didn't come into contact with anyone. We pushed the door open. It led into a dark passage. I felt around for the light switch. Strip lights flickered to life, illuminating a dusty area filled with junk. Old desks, broken chairs, typewriters. But there was a cleared space outside one of the heavy doors that opened off the corridor.

We hurried forward. Aren boosted me up so I could see through the tiny gap in the door.

Charlie was there, pacing back and forth in the cell.

I felt a rush of relief at seeing her. We were really doing this. We were rescuing her.

"Charlie!"

She whirled around, staring up at me in astonishment. "*Matt?*" she said.

Charlie hurried to the door, reaching up to grab my hand through the gap. "What are you doing here?"

I gave her my best heroic smile. "I'm here to rescue you."

She grinned at me. "Aren't you a little short for this?"

I frowned. "I'm not that short!"

She rolled her eyes. "And you call yourself a fan?"

"Huh?"

Then it clicked. Dad would be so disappointed in me. I grinned back and was about to say something devastatingly witty and cool, but just then Aren's legs buckled and I fell from his shoulders, both of us landing in a twisted pile on the floor. The next five minutes were spent trying all the keys in the lock until we found one that fit. We finally got the door open, and Charlie rushed out and grabbed Aren, Calvin, and me into a really tight hug.

"You came back for me," she said.

We finally managed to escape her clutches. "Of course we did," I said. "What else would we do?"

"But time is ticking," said Aren. "We need to move."

We retraced our steps out of the basement and toward the front doors. We could hear the celebrations, the shouting, the—

—the *screaming*?

We looked at each other. That didn't sound good. We moved faster, and as we approached the glass double doors leading out into Edenvale we saw that it really wasn't good.

Not good at all.

A scene of chaos greeted us as we stepped through the doors. People were running in all directions, screaming and shouting. Smoke drifted into the air from what appeared to be a roasted chestnut cart that was on fire. The tent had collapsed. It was like a war zone.

Then we saw them.

Anti-Snuffles and his deadbeat army.

The missing pets were rampaging through the park, hundreds of them, lurching and shuffling after anyone who came close. The deadbeat squirrels were hassling people trying to shelter beneath trees, the squirrels throwing nuts at their heads. Zombie dogs limped and waddled after live cats. I saw a zombie snake that had been cut in half, both halves slithering toward a live hamster that had gotten loose. A deadbeat parrot had landed on the shoulder of what I assume was his old owner. The man was squealing, whirling round in circles as he tried to dislodge the zombie bird, while it squawked, "Who's a pretty boy? Who's a pretty boy?"

And the most bizarre thing of all? The mayor was doing his victory lap around the area where the pet show had been held, totally ignoring the chaos around him. The loudspeaker on his golf cart was blaring out "Circle of Life" from *The Lion King* while a terrified aide stood in the backseat holding Pugsley high in the air, just like the scene from the movie.

Pugsley was wearing a crown.

I turned slowly to Aren, checking if his iPhone was still on his head. "Are you getting all this?"

"Oh yes," said Aren in awe.

A second later Kilgore Dallas appeared in the park, leading the Zombie Squad. They were wearing thick gloves, and they chased after the deadbeat animals, trying to toss them into sacks.

"Come on," I said to Charlie. "We have to get you out of here."

We hurried down the steps. I was about to lead Charlie behind city hall, thinking we could skirt around the park, when she suddenly stopped.

"No."

"No? What do you mean, *no*?"

"Dallas will never catch them. Not before they turn every pet in town."

"So? What can we do about it?"

But it was too late. Charlie was stepping calmly past the screaming townspeople, people who only screamed a lot louder when they saw her. Because, let's face it, you couldn't really mistake her for anything but a zombie now.

We hurried after Charlie. I wasn't sure why, except that we had only gotten the gang back together, and we weren't going to just leave her on her own.

As we drew closer I saw that the mayor's golf cart was being chased by the Rottweiler from the storm drains. Not only that, but Anti-Snuffles was riding on his back.

This was insane. It was like he really was an evil genius, bent on taking over the town.

Anti-Snuffles saw us and dug his little claws into the dog's fur. It skidded to a halt, then turned around.

It started moving toward us. We shrank back, but Charlie didn't move. By this time, Dallas and the Zombie Squad had spotted us as we stood still in the center of the madness. Even a few townspeople who were screaming their lungs out had paused to see what was happening.

The dog came on, snarling and groaning. But I wasn't watching it. I was watching Anti-Snuffles, because his eyes were locked on me.

I swallowed nervously as the dog came within a few feet.

And then Charlie raised a hand and pointed. "NO!" she shouted. "Naughty dog! *Naughty!*"

The dog paused and cocked its head to the side.

"You're a bad doggy! Yes. *Bad!*"

The dog looked around uncertainly. Then it sort of whined. Charlie waited a second, then moved slowly forward with her hand held out. The deadbeat dog sniffed her hand, and Charlie gently stroked its head.

"There, there," she said softly. "You're not a bad dog, are you? You're a good dog."

The dog whined hopefully.

Anti-Snuffles was not happy. He was leaping up and down, chittering noisily in the dog's ear. Eventually, the Rottweiler had had enough, and he shook himself violently. Anti-Snuffles flew up from his perch and sailed through the air, cartwheeling against the blue sky.

I ran. I grabbed an empty sack from Dallas and held it open beneath my hamster. He landed right in it. I snapped the sack shut and breathed a sigh of relief. I had him. I had Anti-Snuffles.

The mayor's golf cart skidded to a halt in front of us. "Circle of Life" stopped suddenly and was replaced by his nasal voice, speaking into the hand mike connected to the loudspeaker.

"Arrest that deadbeat! Arrest her!"

The Zombie Squad made a move toward Charlie, but the Rottweiler turned and growled at them. They stopped moving.

Charlie straightened up and moved toward the golf cart.

"What . . . what are you doing? Don't come any closer! Stay away. That's an order!"

Charlie kept going. The mayor finally dropped the mike and fell out of the cart, scrambling backward across the ground. Charlie climbed into the golf cart.

"You guys coming?" she asked.

"You got a plan?"

"I think so."

So we climbed in, Aren and I in front and Calvin in the back with the terrified aide still holding Pugsley. Charlie put her foot on the pedal, and the cart lurched forward. She picked up the mike and started speaking into it.

"Come on!" she said in a jolly voice. "Come on now. Follow me. There's a good doggy. There's a good pussycat. Come on now. Come on."

As we left the park, Dallas jumped into the back of the cart. It was seriously overloaded now, but it still managed to move forward. Just.

Charlie kept calling the animals through the loudspeaker. And you know what? It was working. I'm not sure if they were responding to her voice or if it was because she was a deadbeat, but the zombie pets were following us.

We were like a horror version of the Pied Piper of Hamelin as the golf cart chugged slowly through the streets of Edenvale, Charlie's voice echoing through the loudspeakers, calling, cajoling, drawing all the deadbeat pets after us.

I looked over my shoulder. They formed a long line behind the golf cart, a trail of zombie animals. And behind them were the townsfolk, following after to see how this was going to end. People were coming out of their houses to see what the noise was all about. I saw Mom and Dad as we passed the house. I waved at them. Dad waved back. Mom just looked at us in astonishment.

But they joined the crowd that followed.

I finally saw where Charlie was taking us. The gates in the wall. They loomed above us as we approached.

She turned to Dallas.

"You better open them."

He nodded, hopping from the golf cart and sprinting ahead.

"You guys better get off now."

"What are you doing?" I asked. Rather stupidly, really. It was pretty obvious what she was doing, but I wanted to hear it from her.

"I'll lead them outside."

"And then?"

"And then . . . and then I don't know," she admitted. She glanced behind us. It looked like the whole town had gathered.

"You're coming back," I said.

"Am I?"

"Yes. Charlie, you are *not* going to ride off into the woods. I'm not getting off this cart until you promise to come back."

"Matt—"

"No. Charlie, I'm serious."

"Me, too," said Aren.

"And me!" said Calvin, raising his hand. He still had the jar attached.

Charlie looked at each of us in turn, then finally threw her hands up in exasperation. "Okay, fine! I promise!"

The gates started to open. I gave her the sack holding Anti-Snuffles, and we hopped off the cart. I felt a twinge of guilt at this. Poor guy. Yes, he was an evil zombie hamster, but he was still my pet. I felt a bit sad to see him go.

Charlie drove on, calling all the pets to follow her. After a few minutes, the last of the deadbeats had crossed over the town boundary.

Charlie kept going till she hit the line of trees in the distance. Then she stopped and got off the cart. I couldn't really see what she was doing, so I ran up the steps to the top of the wall for a better view.

She was petting and stroking the animals. It looked like she was just *talking* to them.

Finally, she straightened up, climbed back into the golf cart, and drove back toward town.

The zombie pets didn't try to follow.

She was about halfway back to us when the mayor arrived, gasping and sweating.

"Shut the gate!" he bellowed. "Quick! Before she gets back in."

Dallas was standing before the gate controls, but the mayor tried to push him out of the way and close the gates. Dallas shoved him back.

"You need to step away, sir," said Dallas.

The mayor looked at him in amazement. "You— you can't do that!" he sputtered. "You can't push *me*. I'm the mayor!" He tried to get past Kilgore again, but this time a few people from the crowd stepped forward to stand in his way.

It was Mom, Dad, and Charlie's mom.

"Move!" screamed the mayor.

"That girl saved our town," said Mom.

"She's not a girl! She's a deadbeat."

"No, she's not," said Dallas. "Leastaways, not the old kind. She's something new."

"I don't care! This is my town, and I will not be ignored!" He tried to push Mom out of the way, but as soon as he laid a hand on Mom, Dad stepped forward, pulled his fist back, and punched the mayor right in the face!

I couldn't believe it! *Dad!*

Of course, the effect *was* ruined a bit when Dad started jumping around, howling in pain and shaking his hand. The mayor, for his part, toppled over and lay unconscious in the street. Pugsley wandered over to the mayor, sniffed him a bit, then cocked his leg and peed on him.

Charlie arrived. She stopped the golf cart outside and looked around shyly, wondering what to expect. Dallas gestured for her to come in, and she broke into a huge smile and gunned the cart through the gates. She got out and stepped over the mayor's prone figure.

Then the crowd broke into cheering. The sound was deafening, a rising tide of goodwill.

I ran down the stairs, and Aren, Calvin, and I raised Charlie onto our shoulders and led her back through the town.

We'd done it. We'd saved Charlie *and* gotten rid of the deadbeat pets.

Achievement unlocked: heroes of the town.

9:00 p.m. And that was our day. I'm now writing this on my bed, watching the news of the great zombie pet trek out of Edenvale. Quite a few people had been filming it, as it turned out. Charlie,

Aren, Calvin, and Katie are playing Runespell, shouting and laughing. Mom used butter to get the mayor's jar off Calvin's hand, and we were all enjoying his candy. It was pretty good.

I threw some candy into my mouth and glanced again at the news. It was the bit where Charlie was coming back to the town after leaving the pets out in the woods.

I was about to turn away and join in Runespell when something made me pause.

I frowned, leaning closer to the television. There was something behind the golf cart, something moving rapidly through the grass as the cart made its way back to the town gates.

I stopped chewing. I couldn't be sure, but it looked . . .

. . . it looked vaguely hamster-shaped.

I had a sudden flash of the movie *The Terminator*, about the nonstop killing machine from the future.

And sure, while I admired the cyborg's tenacity and dedication, I was a *little* bit worried how much Anti-Snuffles took after him.

That he, too, might be back.